"*FROM DARKNESS* i
story that will keep you u
— Shane Gericke,

"*FROM DARKNESS* is gripping from the first pages and leaves you wanting more. I love it!"
— Joan Harris, journalist

"*FROM DARKNESS* is a spine-tingling page-turner with depth. Mysterious, enthralling storytelling."
— Evangeline Johns, author of *The Laser Man*

"*FROM DARKNESS* is hypnotic, a story that pulls you in and won't let go. A truly amazing tale that makes the unbelievable seem all too real."
— Frank Connelly, librarian

"Jacqueline Stigman's *FROM DARKNESS* gets it's hooks into you. And you don't want to be released. I stayed up to 4:30 in the morning to finish it! Didn't want it to end!"
— Anna Grinjesch, The Pesto Queen

"*FROM DARKNESS* weaves a spell, the past providing a key to the present in a haunting and fascinating way, holding the reader from start to finish."
— Howie Firth, Scottish writer & broadcaster

"*FROM DARKNESS* is a book of revelation that crosses overlapping levels of culture, history, and science without ever distancing itself from the truths of the human heart. The story strides from the lyrical to the horrific, laying bare truths about human nature other authors rarely approach. An unforgettable experience."
— Jay Hyams, author of *War Movies, The Life and Times of the Western Movie*, coauthor of *My Time at Tiffany's*, with Gene Moore

For Vivian Patterson
Love,
Jacqueline Stigman
November 5, 2013

FROM
DARKNESS
BOOK ONE
AWAKENING

Find Book 2 - Net of Jewels
at WWW.JACQUELINESTIGMAN.com
or at AMAZON.com

BY JACQUELINE STIGMAN

FROM DARKNESS
BOOK ONE
AWAKENING
January 2013

FROM DARKNESS
BOOK TWO
NET OF JEWELS
February 2013

FROM DARKNESS
BOOK THREE
RETURNNNNN
March 2013

TAROT – TAROT
BOOK ONE
INHERITANCE
October 2013

FROM DARKNESS

BOOK ONE

AWAKENING

JACQUELINE STIGMAN

For my great-grandmother Granny Chapman
who listened to my first stories.

PART ONE

'Lonely and abhorred, I shall consume
to ashes this miserable frame and no longer
feel the agonies that now consume me.'
The Demon was soon borne away by the waves
and lost in the darkness and distance.
Frankenstein
Mary Shelley

Life is more intricate than science will allow.
The Varieties of Religious Experience
William James

Quantum physics shows us that we live in a magical,
miraculous, infinite and eternal realm. We are immersed
in the miraculous, like fish who live their whole lives
unaware of water. We breathe the miraculous. We are
the miraculous. That is the terror. And the rapture.
Ghosts, Magic, and Quantum Physics
Dr. Griffin Digger PhD.

GHOST

It was horribly confusing.

There were so many reflections, like a fun-house mirror.

Sharp white light pierced the shifting darkness. Elusive shadows curled silent as smoke and seas of light burst through walls like waterfalls leaving a tide of greys, a pooling of blacks.

Where was his daughter!

Would he find her in time?

He found he was wearing his favorite suit. From before. And long ago. Still in good condition. That was odd.

All around him people moved like shimmering forms in a slow dance of mysterious purpose, but they couldn't hear or see him. They looked as if they had stepped out of the grainiest photographs, their features faint, the details of their clothing lost. Their voices and every sound around him, as if the whole world were under water.

He tried to find his way among huge nebulous shapes that screamed like rusted metal, moaning like wounded animals as they floated by, eventually realizing they must be buses and trucks.

How could he find his daughter? He was lost. So lost.

And he had been lost, he knew, for a long, long, time.

Here, there was neither left nor right. Here, corners fell away upon approach. Walls turned to smoke, reason to dust.

He walked through doorways and walls. Wandered through a mist of years, with pasts and futures not his own.

He struggled to see through wavering veils that tortured him with their distortions. Where could Julie be?

He found himself on empty stairwells, in rooms he did not recognize, in echoing hallways and quiet dusty attics. Seated on wooden bleachers in the old ball park during a game, in a dark courtroom among the jurors, standing in a crowd as an amusement park barker tried to lure customers into a side-show.

How would he ever find her?

If he remembered his childhood stamp collection, he suddenly found himself falling through an abyss of darkness until he found himself within the stamp he remembered; a beautiful Russian stamp he had treasured.

And there he would float above and about the Madonna and Child. Golden medieval stars piercing the deep blue sky. In the far distance, an ancient dark forest.

His sight was often blurred. Then all at once everything would stand out in unusually sharp focus, and the light would be unnaturally bright but flashing on and off and so fast, as he floated effortlessly over an ordinary, everyday table set for dinner, or someone's back yard with children's swings, or an abandoned railroad yard. But none that looked familiar.

And then, in sudden stops and starts, he would be wrenched forward, by abrupt and irregular increments, until he was staring at a large porcelain mug from half an inch away, recognizing the painted branch of blueberries, painted by his mother, knowing he was back at Norwood again, pulled there by the dark tide of his longing and grief, anger and regret.

His life repeated itself over and over.

He was alone in a row boat, happily fishing in the middle of a still lake at dawn. He lay wounded in great pain with other soldiers on a plane bound for a hospital. Home on leave, he smiled at his sleeping baby daughter for the first time. Again and again, he would arrive at the same bus barn he had returned to at the end of his shift, on so many sub-zero nights in Chicago, so long ago. Once, he found himself in his grave.

Oh, Julie, how will I ever find you? Where can you be?

He cried out in utter frustration. He moved at the speed of thought while everyone and everything moved so slowly he felt unbearably alien and alone. His cry echoed as if he shouted into the deepest well, then flew away from him, swallowed whole in the agonizing never ending twilight.

It was so easy to return to the past.

So hard to find the present.

But he must find her. He must!

And if he did, how she must hate him after all these years.

Torn from within, pulled from without, he could only keep searching. He would ask someone, call to them or tap them on their shoulder, his voice echoing in the thick air that lapped about him.

But they rarely heard him nor felt his touch.

A few looked about them, shivered, and hurried away.

He had to find her. He couldn't fail her again! Not this time!

For brief moments he would forget everything, and feel great joy and delight and elation. Then he would remember how he had unwittingly abandoned his wife, his daughter, and his mother and father, and be plunged back into a wild and limitless sorrow.

Knowing his daughter was in the gravest danger, and he, the only one who knew.

ONE

NEW YORK CITY 2:11 A.M.

In Manhattan, an early December fog mixed with snow blew in off the Hudson River and across the West Side Highway, flying inland along the waterfront lanes and glistening cobblestone alleys.

Only a few blocks uptown, the Empire State Building rose out of the mist glowing deep blue and soft white. While just downtown in Chelsea, the flame of a nineteenth century gas lamp burning at the foot of a brownstone's stairs, flickers through the veil of falling snow.

On West Twenty-ninth, between OTB and a Chinese-Cuban diner in an old three-story building, in a raw warehouse space, a young woman is sleeping fitfully on a tattered couch. Tangled in an old army blanket, it looks like she's trying, unsuccessfully, to wake from a very bad dream.

She was so large, too large, struggling forward, one heavy foot, then the other. As if this were not her own body she inhabited, as if she wore an unbearably heavy costume she could neither escape nor remove.

Trapped inside a large ungainly thing, she stumbled and staggered, her hands, wrists and arms slashed and bleeding and so badly mended with clumsy stitches of coarse black string, so knotted and twisted and tangled, the bloody wounds gaped.

On the couch, the young woman struggles desperately, moaning in sick terror, and with clenched fists and a strangled cry she suddenly bolts upright. Eyes wide but not yet fully awake.

Heart pounding, gulping for air, she lunged in the darkness for her lamp, nearly knocking it over, switching it on.

The lamp cast a halo of warm yellow light, but it was not a comfort.

Julie Norwood stared at her shaking hands. Turned them over, back and forth. Quickly explored her face, as if she were blind. And burst into tears.

She shoved the sleeves of her sweatshirt up to her elbows, gasping as she watched her nightmare's bloody wounds slowly fade, and the old scars that never would.

In full panic now, her arms locked around her knees, every muscle unbearably tense, still under the nightmare's eerie spell, she began to rock back and forth whimpering, sounding even to herself like a wounded animal. Writing in her journal could not help her now.

Waking in terror, desperate to throw off the dread that still clung to her, more than anything she wanted to call her best friend.

She pulled her phone out of her jean's pocket, saw the time, and slipped it back in her pocket. It was almost two-thirty in the morning. Lorraine wouldn't mind, but she would wake Max too.

No, she would handle her terror and despair, for one more night, the only way she knew how.

On a paint-stained wooden table near the two large windows, tubes of oil paint and brushes lay scattered across an open sketch pad covered with paint smudged drawings, color chalks and pencils, and chunks of soft vine charcoal. A prepared canvas, four feet square, stood propped on two gallon cans of turp, leaning against a wall.

She rubbed away her tears.

Took a deep breath.

. . . slashed and bleeding, ugly stitches of coarse black string, knotted and twisted and tangled, bloody wounds gaping . . .

She dreamed she was a monster. Every night.

A monstrous girl pieced together badly.

Her soul a sharp bright flame imprisoned in something dead.

Jesus.

Angry at the nightmare that had stalked her since childhood and now still stalking around in her head, she kicked her way out of her tangled blanket and got up off the couch wearing black jeans, and a black t-shirt under a grey sweat shirt, all spattered with dried paint.

She slept in her socks, too, so she slipped right into an old pair of sneakers she left at the loft.

Walking over to her work table, she dug in one of her pockets for a black elastic band, to pull her long wavy sleep tangled hair out of her way.

In the shadows, finished paintings leaned against three walls.

She pulled a cardboard box out from under her work-table. Removed the tall votive candles and arranged them in a wide half circle in front of the canvas. Reached for a box of matches and lit them all. Aimed a small spotlight at the canvas. Switched it on.

Forced another deep breath.

No thoughts

A way to survive she found long ago.

No thoughts

Even so, Ed skittered across her mind.

Not now!

She drifted back to the table. Squeezed several mounds of paint onto a paper palette. Chose a brush. Found a rag.

You are a monstrous girl pieced together badly!

Julie looked up at the ceiling in shadow, the candlelight flickering across her face. "Stop it!" Stop what? Who?

With one more deep shuddering breath, she stepped inside the half ring of burning candles, palette in one hand, paint brush in the other.

Eyes closed, tears spilling down her cheeks, seeking comfort yet again in work, her face a mask of pain.

TWO

ED

Women are such easy prey.

Dinner, flowers, a gift or two, it was only a matter of time, before he had them exactly where he wanted them.

Julie Norwood, however, was different.

Two weeks ago, when they met at the Metropolitan Museum of Art, he felt he knew her. A slender pale brunette. So like mother, when mother was young. And after two dinner dates, she had not invited so much as a good night kiss.

Extraordinary!

A lovely irresistible challenge.

Inspiring, really.

She was the one.

Deliciously obstinate, he looked forward to correcting her when she became part of his Persephone Project, already begun in a small way.

Smiling at his private joke, he winced with pain. His lips always so chapped they bled. His tongue darted in and out, licking the blood. He staunched the bleeding quickly with a white linen handkerchief.

The mutant genius in a family from upstate New York, Ed resembled his father, with his flaxen hair and large bones. But his mother had forgiven him that. He had his father's eyes as well. A pale blue that conveyed a false mildness. From his mother, he inherited a sensuous iron will. His powerful body, molded by years of lifting weights, entirely his own creation.

Dr. Edward Henry, research scientist at The Scientific Studies Institute of New York, surveyed his gleaming instruments, methodically arranged on metal trays.

His subject's screams during the day would have brought interference. So he worked at night, when no one could stop him.

The beauty of secrecy and the utter sensuality of complete authority gave him the freedom to do as he pleased.

In a Plexiglass cage, a young Rhesus monkey, bolted into place by steel cuffs and collar, a nightmare nest of electrodes driven into his exposed brain, stared at Ed, knowing the agony to come.

Ed smiled, quoting aloud from *The Island of Dr. Moreau*: "The thing before you is no longer an animal, a fellow creature, but a problem." *Thank you Dr. Moreau and your screaming puma!*

But people were squeamish these days. Therefore, privacy was fundamental. Only with privacy assured might he leap beyond the quagmire of their irrelevant ethical systems, cutting ruthlessly into obstinate flesh, demanding the knowledge that lay buried like treasure, hidden within that filthy stronghold.

Flesh was dumb, but he could make it speak.

It would tell him anything he wanted to know, eventually.

Ed smiled at the monkey. "Ready to go to work?"

The monkey stared at him, unable to move.

Ed sighed. Once, he'd had rooms full of primates, cats, and dogs. But working with lower life forms no longer excited him. He had moved on, and apparently, there was no going back.

He would have this animal trashed tomorrow. He could no longer tolerate the sight or smell of it. Never could actually. They were always a means to an end: his ongoing study of intense isolation and pain.

Eager now, he locked the lab. Entered the elevator. Inserted a key and pushed the Sub 2 button.

For years, he had suffered intolerable interruptions from prying students, techs, and colleagues, even at night. But now, he had a secret lab. Found and renovated by the night guard, Lyle Oldman, a creature who knew better than to question.

The Institute, built in 1897, gated with stationed guards and hidden within a public park far uptown, stood along the shore of the East River.

For decades, the Sub 2 basement level had been used to store damaged, discarded, or obsolete equipment. However, the East River's eventual invasion ended all that some time ago. Most of the corridors and rooms were flooded a foot deep, the water swimming with the occasional fish, and littered with urban debris.

Further flooding had been checked, and the Sub 2 sealed. Elevators no longer descended to that level. Until Lyle ferreted out an old elevator key. The creature was proving useful. Should he prove disloyal, in any way, the tunnel in the Sub 2 leading to the river would prove convenient.

No one could predict Ed's moods lately, not even himself. His headaches were becoming more frequent, but he knew they were a function of the needless obstacles he encountered.

On a bad day, if you were nobody, God help you.

But then, Ed mused, everyone was nobody.

Except Julie.

Lyle found one of the few unflooded rooms, apparently on higher ground. People were often unaware that Manhattan had originally been quite hilly.

He then installed a new door of case hardened steel, hidden behind a rusted steel shelving unit, that now slid aside on an embedded track he also installed. Clever trick. Good monkey.

Ed made his way through the flooded twisting tunnels on planks laid on cinderblocks, then slid the shelving unit aside, unlocked the steel door, and entered his secret dimly lit lab.

As always, the sight of the cage took his breath away.

Everything in the lab was white or stainless steel.

Except the cage.

In the dim light, the three foot tall black iron triangular dungeon hulked on the shining steel table like a time travelling tool of medieval torture.

A narrow grate along its base the only opening, except for a catch-all on the bottom for droppings.

Harry Harlow, the scientist who invented this experimental device in the 1970s, called it The Pit of Despair.

Ed switched his flashlight on low and approached the cage. Behind the grate, two little bare feet lay twined about each other.

Persephone appeared to be sleeping.

THREE

KEEPSAKE

Julie woke up on the floor shivering.

The old army blanket slipping off her bare shoulder as she stirred, still half asleep, she lifted her head slowly, opened her eyes, and sat up fast.

Fear jolting through her she stared in stunned disbelief at the streaks of black, white, and fiery orange paint, whipping around her bare thighs, across her hips and belly, over her bare breasts.

Even more terrifying, she didn't remember taking off her clothes, or even painting.

Although her brushes loaded with paint lay scattered around her on the floor, and her palette, the pigment blurred like a small abstract painting, lay within arm's reach.

With an ominous feeling of foreboding, she looked up at the canvas she had been about to paint last night and gasped.

Where did that come from?

Standing up slowly, the blanket forgotten slipping to the floor, her long dark hair cascading over her pale shoulders and down her back, she stared at her night's work.

She had painted the face of a young girl in profile against a stormy grey background. A girl with bright orange hair streaming behind her. So bright and glowing, her hair reminded of stained glass bathed in molten sunlight.

No. *See what you painted.*

Julie's paint-stained hand covered her mouth as she moaned.

The girl's hair was on fire!

Her face, grey as an ancient Greek statue riddled with white cracks. Her eye, a white gleaming oval. Her soft young mouth open in a silent scream.

Like an entranced sleepwalker, Julie walked up to the canvas slowly. Bent down, picked up a brush, and with the tip of its wooden handle, she scratched across the white cracks on the grey face, the paint still wet, making lines that looked like stitches. Stitches twisting this way and that.

She'd painted a young dead girl screaming.

A monstrous girl pieced together badly.

Julie dropped the brush and backed away from the painting.

It was too early on a cold morning, when you've obviously been up all night doing things you don't even remember, to wake up and face the fact that you might be losing your mind.

Might?

A picture could be worth a thousand words, or a thousand hours talking to a shrink. But she was not willing to spend another minute staring at what she knew had to be her own terrifying self-portrait.

Grabbing her clothes off the floor she pulled them on fast. She'd clean the paint off later. She patted her back pocket. Her phone still there.

At the small table where she kept her tea things and snacks, she poured bottled water into an electric kettle, pressed the button, then glanced at a museum postcard of St. George slaying the Dragon taped to the wall, next to a framed photo of her father in his army uniform. His arm around a buddy. She kissed her fingers and pressed them to her father's photo. "Morning, dad."

Still shivering, she reached over and switched the space heater to HIGH.

Back on the couch, wrapped in the blanket, her knees drawn up close to her, she sipped her steaming mug of black China tea.

Opening the box of chocolate donuts resting in her lap, she eyed the new painting warily.

The nightmare kept creeping up on her, too, but she pushed it away—hard. And she didn't want to think about what the painting might mean.

A young dead girl screaming. *Christ.*

Instead, she sipped her hot tea, and took a bite of the chocolate donut and tried to think.

Why had she taken off her clothes? No idea. Why had she painted all over her body? Didn't make any sense. And why didn't she remember doing any of that? She didn't even remember doing the painting!

And then there's the nightmare she's had since childhood that now has a new bonus feature! It doesn't quit when she wakes up! At least not for a few agonizing seconds.

Her hand trembled as she raised the donut to her mouth and paused. She must be going crazy. Really. Losing her mind. Seriously.

What other explanation could there be?

But why? And why now? None of this made sense.

She finished the donut, and reached for another, surveying the loft she rented five months ago.

The windows were old and warped and wouldn't close, so they let in the rain and didn't keep out the cold. The bathroom fixtures looked like they dated from 1910. And there were mice. At least, one. Grey and so tiny, with big soft Mickey Mouse ears. She couldn't bear to set traps.

When she rented the loft in July, men working in the warehouse across the street were taking coffee breaks at their window watching her paint. She couldn't work that way.

So she covered both windows, with white plastic shower curtains she found cheap on Canal and stapled them together.

After she hung her "drapes," she loved how daylight filtering through the white plastic filled the loft with a diffused white light creating the impression of a timeless, nearly lunar solitude.

The only real problem was the rent. Money was tight, but she got enough freelance graphic design to pay the bills, and the rent was lower than other lofts she'd seen, probably because of the shape it was in.

When Gran offered to help, she had thanked her, but refused. She was nineteen and taking on the expense of a loft was her idea. She had planned coming to New York to paint for a long time.

Working hard and taking classes straight through every summer with overloaded schedules, she finished high school at fifteen. College at eighteen.

Why the rush?

She told Gran she loved to paint, and there were so many museums and galleries in New York, why wait?

But Julie knew her wanting to get started as soon as possible had more to do with her family history: her father disappeared one night when she was six. Two years later her mother died unusually young of a stroke. So Julie felt she learned very early that you can't count on much and you don't know how long you've got.

She would try it for a year. She didn't know exactly what she wanted to do with her life. She knew that worried Gran, but she just didn't know yet. She did know she loved to paint!

And now, she had a painting space with plenty of north light.

She had been painting in her two room apartment, since she came to New York right after college last year, after majoring in Comparative Religion because of all the wonderful art from all over the world, and because of the mystery, the symbols and stories, and what she thought of as one of our most deeply felt feelings, our longing for the Divine.

She also minored with a heavy load of Graphic Design. Planning to move to New York she knew she would need a way to make a living.

As soon as she got here, about a year ago, she began looking for a gallery to show them the paintings she had done so far. Trying to overcome her nearly crippling shyness.

And now, having a loft, when an art dealer made the rare studio visit to see her paintings, she greeted them at the door trying to ignore her pounding heart.

It was an old struggle for her, wanting to show her work, but desperately needing to hide.

Whatever she chose to do with her life she would have to get over that.

All she had to do was be herself. Why was that so hard?

Despite her fear, after showing her work to one dealer after another, she'd finally been included in a small group show in a new gallery on the lower East Side. She'd been ecstatic!

Because of the show, several dealers made studio visits and complimented her work. But none offered her a show.

Why? She knew.

You're not good enough.

Face it.

Knowing she was overreacting, she hadn't shown her new work to anyone. Why was she so afraid?

No mystery. She knew that, too.

Nothing she ever did felt good enough.

She knew she should believe in herself no matter what, but when your father leaves you behind, and never comes back, it's hard to believe you're worth anything at all.

Julie sipped her tea. Where is he now, she wondered, heart aching, remembering one night, when she must have been about three years old.

The sound of grown-ups laughing woke her. She'd managed to climb out of her crib and follow the voices to the living room where her mother and father were visiting with neighbors. They invited her in, but she'd stayed just outside the room, still half-asleep.

"She's shy," she heard her mother say.

The neighbors smiled.

"You'll take her?" she heard her mother ask.

Her daddy stood up and stubbed out his cigarette. Smiling at her as he swooped her up in his arms, he carried her back to bed where he tucked an empty matchbook cover that glowed in the dark into her little hand, a comfort he knew she needed against the darkness. Dominos on the cover gleamed in the night as she lay in her crib drifting off to sleep.

Her father's sudden disappearance, so long ago, was a wound that never healed. "It's *freezing* in here!" she said, chopping at the blanket with the blade of her hand, jabbing it under her, trying and failing, to keep out the chill, and the relentless sorrow.

She pulled out her phone and checked the time: 6:30am.

Sam would be opening up soon.

The owner of All Trades, Sam was a lively man who looked twenty years younger than his eighty-five, stood about five-foot-three, and worked six days a week, from seven in the morning to seven at night.

Although bewildered by his wife's recent death, he had taken a friendly and protective interest in Julie, bringing her mouse traps, plastic boxes, anything he thought she could use. In turn, she brought him some of her homemade oatmeal raisin cookies, but he had patted his round stomach and said he was watching his weight. Eventually, she learned from his friend Sy, that he liked the sweet and sour soup from down the block, so she picked some up for him every now and then.

All Trades Employment for day-workers, just across the hall from her loft, opened at seven. And just about then, the sounds of trucks backing up, honking horns, drivers yelling and slamming their doors would start just outside her window, the street one floor below.

To avoid the racket during the day, whenever her freelance schedule allowed, she stayed over at the loft. When the tiny local eateries and warehouses closed, and the street became so beautifully quiet and deserted, she would listen to some jazz, some Mississippi Blues, and then Bach's Toccata and Fugue in D minor as she painted long into the night, drinking endless cups of tea.

In the luminous solitude and silence she worked well, her mind slowly letting go of her usual concerns and opening like a flower, like a many petaled lotus, opening to the mystery and power of inspiration. And then she would play the sensuous luscious nature of the glistening oil paint against the mysterious emptiness of the bare white canvas, striving to ignite color and feeling, searching for the visions that were hers alone.

And then, the paint and canvas would become a net for catching the wordless hidden heart of things, that she would try, like so many before her, to render in paint. Van Gogh and Monet had succeeded. Vermeer, too.

Lately, she had been painting mummies. She thought them powerful and even beautiful. Although Lorraine had felt free to inform her that it was no wonder none of the galleries were interested. She wouldn't want a mummy hanging over her couch.

Julie smiled, at the thought of her friend, and finished her tea. Time to work.

But first a quick trip to the chilly bathroom to relieve herself and splash some cold water on her face. An old mirror over the tiny sink, having lost much of its silver, covered her reflection with black lace as she watched herself brush her teeth, and the fluorescent light flickered and buzzed overhead like a signal from the Twilight Zone.

Her phone trilled. She pulled it out and checked. Ed. A man she met recently and had dinner with twice. Who made her feel uneasy. Calling her at seven in the morning? She slid her phone back in her pocket. Yanked the overhead string that turned off the light and left the room.

Headed toward her work table. Working, she could forget almost anything, until the hours of solitude woke the feelings of loss and sorrow that haunted her like lonely ghosts.

How much she missed her father, even after all these years. Her sorrow and unanswered questions still tormenting her: Where is he now? Is he still alive? Or was it too late? Why did he leave?

She was no longer surprised that her sorrow was as raw as it ever was. She just tried not to think about him. There was so much not to think about. The pain locked away, her grief buried deep.

She wouldn't let herself get mired in self-pity. The world was full of horrors, of war and famine and plague.

Children were abandoned every day. Everyone knew that. Everyone but the kids left behind. She had a wound that never healed, but she'd learned to live with it.

Oh? What about that nightmare that keeps coming back? Those bloody wounds all over your body sewn together with childish stitches knotted and twisted and tangled?

And what about the young dead girl you painted last night? Her hair on fire, her soft young mouth open in a scream?

Julie knew she needed to work right now, needed the forgetfulness work would bring. But before she could act her parched heart whispered—

You monster. Who wouldn't leave you!

Her head swung aside, as if slapped.

"*Stop it!*" Stop what? Who?

Talking to herself. No, she wasn't. She was talking to someone. She just didn't know who.

She glared at the painting of the young dead girl screaming.

Sucked in a deep breath and sat down on a stool with a round wooden seat and an iron base, she'd salvaged from the street one night.

She slipped her phone out of her back pocket and lay it down on her work table, out of the way, but within reach.

On her table, under the sketch pad, she found what she was looking for: a thick folder stained with oil paint. She opened it and spread out the contents of her image file.

These were pictures she had torn from magazines, books, and newspapers, and some photos she'd taken. Like this one shot from the roof of her tenement building early one misty morning, of water towers on the roofs of old buildings in the distance, haunting, stark, and medieval.

And maps. She loved searching through the bins of old book stores, for maps of the ancient world—Cathay, Byzantium, Sibir and Tebeth! She especially loved the vast unexplored territories of antique maps—Marco Polo's *Region of Darkness*, and *Shambhala*. She longed to travel, to see Paris, Venice, and the pyramids! Well, she wanted to see the world. And promised herself she would, someday, somehow.

On her work table and along her shelves, she collected small objects she found on the street, or in some odd little shop: a thimble from an old monopoly game, a faded puzzle piece, a broken toy compass. Even a coverless book of matches spread like a fan, found at the edge of a puddle, the phosphorous and ink washed away by the rain, pale purple, nearly gone to white, but it didn't glow in the dark.

Julie was drifting now. Her burnt sienna brown eyes, no longer focused in the here-and-now, searched a farther, further inner distance.

Her breathing slowed and her eyes darkened, as she picked up something from the table and passed it from one hand to the other, back and forth, unconsciously.

In the street, someone leaned on a horn and she jumped. Discovering what she held in her hand. A gift from her mother.

It reminded her in a way of an Easter egg toy her father had once shown her. Saved by Gran from his childhood.

A little larger than a young child's hand, it looked as if it were iced like a cake, sparkling with pink flowers and pale green leaves.

At one end, a small circular window, the size of a dime, and when you looked inside you saw paper cutout rabbits and chicks in the cellophane grass among pastel paper flowers.

That something contained the entirely unexpected, that things were not what they seemed, was fascinating yet frightening to her as a child.

Like a brightly colored terrifying Jack-in-the-Box, that she did not want to open.

A hidden world reminded her of something important she needed to remember, but never could. And in her heart she knew her forgetfulness, that mysterious fading away of her own inner map, was all her fault. As if she was doing it on purpose.

But what if the thing forgotten was buried for a reason? What if this buried thing wasn't treasure? Julie shuddered, then looked down at her mother's gift.

In her palm, she held what looked, at first glance, like an open shell—but within, someone had carved a miniature Chinese landscape. A world within a world her mother gave her for her seventh birthday, soon after her father disappeared.

For Julie, the gift became a keepsake, a memento that marked the end of her childhood.

The shell weighed heavily in her hand. Old, elaborately carved ivory, it came from Norwood, her grandmother's home, her father's boyhood home, named for Nathan Norwood, the ancestor who settled the land long ago.

On top of the shell, carved in lavish relief, a burly dragon soared in a swirling storm of clouds, gripping the earth in five curling yellow claws.

Bushy eyebrows twisting wildly and smoke streaming from his flared nostrils made him look fierce, she had always concluded, but not mean. An ancient guardian holding the earth firmly in place, keeping it safe amid the pandemonium of life.

For within the shell, all was peaceful.

Carved inside, a tiny thatched cottage stood beside a tall pine tree, whose twisting trunk seemed to be dancing, even as it sheltered with its broad branches.

In front of the cottage and under the tree, a child stood, one arm raised forever in greeting, standing next to a man and woman who appeared to be the child's mother and father.

In front of them, a river with a strongly carved current flowed around the side of the cottage, where it surged beneath a waterwheel (that turned if you touched it) and out of sight.

A low foot-bridge spanned the river in front of the waterwheel. While coursing upriver, a sampan at full sail was about to collide with a duck that swam downstream.

Of course, the duck might swim out of harm's way, or the boat steer around it, but then the sampan would surely crash through the footbridge.

But, no. All these years, within the shell, the child continued to wave, the duck swam, the sampan sailed. The mother and father did not disappear. And within, all remained peaceful.

The dragon soaring over all holding the world firmly in place.

After her father left that night and then disappeared, no one knowing what happened to him, she'd lived in fear.

Maybe that was why she held on to things too long. And when she finally did let go of something, she'd wish she hadn't. Because it was usually impossible to retrieve what she had thrown away.

Who can?

When her father walked out to their car that spring night did he know he would never return?

When he came into her bedroom wearing his overcoat, carrying his hat, she pretended to be asleep.

She was six years old and very angry.

She heard her mother and father arguing and that frightened her. Now he was going out. She didn't want him to leave. It was night time. Time to go to sleep.

So she pretended to be asleep when he whispered, "Princess?"

He'd bent down and kissed her cheek, but she didn't open her eyes.

In the dark she heard him sigh. And then leave.

She never saw him again.

What had he wanted to tell her?

She always wondered, all those nights when she cried herself to sleep with missing him, what would have happened if she had thrown her small arms around her father's neck and begged him not to go. Or cried out, *Take me with you!*

Instead, when she heard the front door slam, she jumped out of bed and stood by the window, tears rolling down her cheeks as she watched him get in the car, pull out of the driveway, then drive slowly up the street and into the night forever.

Julie stroked the dragon's back, as if to summon a genie, wishing what she always wished, whispering in the empty loft, *"Please come back."*

Why didn't he come back?

Hot tears fell again, tortured by the answer her broken heart feared most: *He didn't love you.*

Her phone. Echoing in the loft. Where was it?

"Pearl! What" . . . "What?" . . . "I'll come home right away!" . . . "Oh. With snow, hard to say". . . "As soon as I can" . . . "Can you stay until" . . . "What did Dr. Blum say?" . . . "Oh, God.". . . "Tell Gran I'll be there tonight. And tell her I love her!" . . . "You, too, Pearl. Bye."

Julie frowned at something on the floor. No wonder it was so cold! A window must have blown open a little during the night leaving a small drift of dirty snow.

Her grandmother had had a heart attack. No cause for worry, the doctor said. Just come home as soon as you can.

Julie rushed at the window and slammed it shut.

Kicked at the snow. Then lifted the white plastic away from the window to look outside.

It was still snowing. The street, deserted. Except for one lone man walking by on the other side of the street wearing a long dark coat and fedora. He turned his head and looked at her. Inclined his head and touched the rim of his hat.

She raced to her door, tore at the lock, nearly fell down the stairs to the street. Yanked the front door open, ran out on the sidewalk, stood in the cold staring.

Gone.

Shaken, shivering, angry and disappointed, she stomped up the steep stairs to the loft, remembering all the other times she thought she'd seen her father. Thought he had returned and would finally explain everything.

She would see him riding by in a car or driving a bus as he used to. In the subway, or a crowd. Today, for the first time, walking by her loft. Each time, he turned toward her for one timeless moment, and she knew he saw her. Then he would disappear into thin air.

A cruel trick of the mind. Like the child she heard crying in the apartment on the floor above her loft, although she'd never met the tenant. And she had not investigated or reported what she heard because it was the same child crying she heard in her own apartment building.

Sometimes the crying seemed to come from the building attached to hers. Sometimes from a wall that she shared with the next apartment. Sometimes from the floor below as she lay down on the carpet to listen. Sometimes from above her apartment.

That was especially scary because her apartment was on the tenement's top floor.

She didn't know why, and it seemed like a terrible thing to admit even to herself, but the child crying did not make her feel any sympathy. It only made her angry. Especially since it followed her home and then again back to the loft.

A crying, miserable ghost child following her around and all she could feel was anger. Or was it fear? Because she probably didn't like even more evidence that she was going crazy.

At home she sometimes shouted "Go away!" Squeezed pillows against her ears until it did. And then the guilt and feelings of loss and self-judgment would descend.

Haunted by her recurring horrific nightmare and a crying ghost child (what else to call it?), not to mention her father's fleeting apparitions, she had begun to feel she might be losing her mind, even before the events of last night.

Why? Again, she had no idea.

So she did what she usually did, she ignored what terrified her as best she could.

But she couldn't think of her father or her nightmares, or the crying ghost child now. She had to get to Norwood.

Still, she stood there, as a chill fell lightly over her shoulders like a silken cloak of gentle snow. Death's most tender warning touch.

Finally, she had to force herself to move, to break its spell. In ten minutes, she alerted the alarm company, locked up, and grabbed a cab heading for her apartment to pack.

In the abandoned loft, the ivory shell lay forgotten, a mystery unseen.

For within the shell, an unleashed blizzard drove drifts of snow against the tiny cottage, and the river had turned to ice. The water wheel careened, frozen in place. The sampan's sail had become an ice encrusted torn grey shroud. The duck lay on the frozen river its feet bound in icy shackles.

The child's cry lost in the shriek of arctic winds. The mother and father gone.

FOUR

BLOODY PIECES

Ed locked the door to his secret lab and began to make his way out of the Sub 2, smiling.

Dr. Edward Henry was a man of fierce ambition, but in the history of his field, he was filled with admiration for Dr. Harry Harlow, the inventor of The Pit of Despair, who had described his work as experimental studies of affection, love, and bonding.

Many just called him cruel.

In the 1970's, Harlow became known for these experiments with rhesus macaque monkeys; a species known to be tough and independent, yet intensely social, and desperate in loneliness.

Harlow was quoted saying, "You know, I like to grab people's attention." And he did.

Working at the University of Wisconsin at Madison, he devised experiments to study the effects of isolation on infant rhesus monkeys, taking them from their mothers and imprisoning them in a vertical triangular isolation chamber he designed and named, The Pit of Despair.

Monkeys held in this apparatus saw only the hands of those who fed them and cleaned their "cage." Harlow kept monkeys in The Pit of Despair as long as two years.

Ed had nothing but respect for this man who had been forced to contend with petty criticism.

True, the animals confined to the Pit of Despair, even for short periods of time, ceased to be monkeys; emerging socially and mentally destroyed. Most unable to eat or drink any longer.

But then, the weakness in Harlow's work was obvious. If researchers were to learn anything significant, they must work with humans, regardless of sentimentality. Why not put our strays to good use?

Ed reached the elevator and unlocked it, smiling again, as he remembered having Harlow's chamber reproduced.

The originals having been destroyed after Harlow's death by small-minded colleagues.

However, logic and daring inspired Ed to plan a much more exciting experiment, one the romantic in him called— The Persephone Project. To accommodate his subject, the Pit of Despair had been made a bit larger, but not much.

And in his secret lab, no one could stop him.

Inside the elevator, Ed noticed a poster announcing an Animal Rights demonstration. Animal Rights! Women's Rights! Ha! These people knew nothing! Nothing! And they would judge science? And want to run the world? Ha!

What right did they have to any say about the work being carried on at the Institute? Telling scientists how to work. Certainly! By all means!

The demonstration occurred last week. Lyle told him they forced their way into the Institute, aiming their camcorders, shouting slogans, wildly intent on documenting animal abuse.

They didn't know where to look. They never found any of the labs, much less his. And they would never find it. He had outsmarted them.

He had outsmarted them all.

Harlow made the mistake of revealing his work to the public.

Ed never would.

For he knew, if the demonstrators discovered his Persephone Project, they would forget about animal rights and tear him to bloody pieces.

FIVE

A COLD FIST

On her way home in the cab, staring out at the whirling snow, Julie shivered with bone chilling fear, followed fast by a flood of shame, because the fear she felt wasn't only for Gran, but for herself as well.

When Gran died, she would be completely alone.

After her father disappeared, Julie remembered watching the world as if through a grey curtain. When her grades fell, her teacher wrote on her first grade report card, "She's not here."

Two years later, her mother died suddenly. Unusually young for a stroke. Sitting in the funeral home at the wake, the intense scent of flowers flooding the room, Julie sat beside her grandmother, Louise Merchant Norwood, holding tight to the elder woman's firm, loving hand.

The day after the funeral, Julie and Gran flew back to Norwood, Massachusetts, where they began their new life together. Even so, behind the grey curtain, Julie wandered more lost than ever before.

It was snowing even harder when the cab came to a stop in front of the well-kept tenement in the east seventies where Julie lived.

Lorraine said her two room apartment reminded her of a cross between a country cabin and a nineteenth century townhouse given the chocolate brown velvet drapes she made herself and the wooden furniture she bought from second-hand stores and refinished. The Welsh nineteenth century hutch for the kitchen, a church pew chair of solid mahogany with carved lion feet, and a rolled top desk she loved in the living room had been her rewards, when she had a particularly grueling schedule of graphic design.

She brought a couple of worn antique throw rugs from Norwood, and hung some of her smaller paintings, along with framed prints of Dickens, Buddha, Shakespeare, and the Hindu goddess Kali, who stuck out her tongue, appeared to be dancing, and wore an apron of severed arms and a necklace of skulls. An image that appealed to her for some reason.

When Lorraine saw it she frowned and muttered, "You might consider hiding her if you ever invite a date up here."

Any remaining space was filled with a twin sized bed, a small table and chairs, two silver finish metal lamps that looked slightly space age, unmatched bookcases overflowing with books, art magazines, CDs, DVDs, and her *Ficus Benjamina* tree about to outgrow its window.

A photo of Gran and several of her dad were arranged on her bureau. And now that she had the loft to paint in, she had room for a couch. Her small place was crowded but looked and felt good to her. It was home.

Worried about Gran, Julie pulled off her painting clothes, wiped off the paint with a can of turp she kept at home, for small clean ups, and hurried through a shower.

Afterward, she dressed warmly in black corduroys, a grey turtle neck sweater, and a black pull-over, guessing the bus would be cold. In the back of her closet she dug out her snow boots.

And packed quickly. Ready to go, she looked outside. The snow storm a blizzard now, she began to wonder what the roads would be like, not looking forward to hurtling along icy highways in a bus all the way up to Norwood, Massachusetts. The sooner she got going the better. She'd call Lorraine when she got there.

Her closest friend, Lorraine O'Connor, was the best. Warm, loyal, savvy and fun. A few years older than Julie, a textile designer, and already happily married to a wonderful guy, Julie loved her and treasured their friendship, especially since she'd never made friends easily, and found it hard to trust.

Why let anyone close? They leave you or die.

Even so, she felt an abiding guilt, as if she deserved her isolation; that it was a punishment, and she should know she had gotten off easy.

When Gran died, there would be no family. No family, and no desire to ever marry. She had her art. That was enough.

Except she couldn't imagine what she would do without Gran. And she had spent so little time up at Norwood since she moved to the city!

Julie zipped her backpack shut with unnecessary force as feelings of fear and regret hit so hard she stumbled.

The snow storm rattled her tenement windows, as she felt death's cold fist clutch her heart and squeeze possessively.

She had to get going, now.

Just as she was leaving, she heard the ghost child weeping.

She knew there weren't any young children in apartments near hers. And even if there were, that wouldn't explain why it followed her around.

Not now. This is too much.

She always felt a crushing feeling of guilt for ignoring it's pain. But what could she do?

She moved quickly now. Grabbed her keys, slipped into her backpack, shouldered her bag. At the door she looked back.

Her furniture, books, and even her paintings, suddenly looked strangely unfamiliar. As if they belonged to someone she once knew, but no longer.

SIX

CARAVAN OF WHISPERERS

Maneuvering through the crowd inside the Port Authority Bus Terminal, Julie spotted the ticket windows up ahead. But just then, a lost caravan of two came stumbling across her path like a kinetic mirage.

Julie stopped and stared. She wasn't the only one. A crowd gathered mesmerized by the startling side-show.

Two men shambled forward like sleepwalkers. Youth led age, both whispering intently under their breath. Bare-chested, dirty wash pants hung low, skin pale and sweaty, eyes barely open.

Like an altar boy, the young man led the procession, ringing a gently *chirring* bell, the kind usually clamped on a tricycle's handlebars. The boy had quite a few tattoos up and down his arms, but the middle-aged high priest shambling behind his acolyte appeared a living tapestry. Tattoos cavorted across his chest, danced up and down his arms and back, encircled his neck, jeweled his hands.

A wildly cheerful Felix the Cat skipped by a picturesque ship at sea in full sail. A voluptuous naked lady displayed her charms, unaware of a leering joker and *MOM* inscribed on a banner in Victorian script. The man's chest and shoulders mobbed with a patriotic eagle, an American flag, a spider with its perfect web dangling over a large pink rose, and a grinning skull wearing a jaunty black top-hat smoking a cigarette.

Dominoes and dice, hearts and diamonds, clubs and spades skipped up and down both arms. Dracula in a swirling black cape flew across his back. A golden carp and pink peonies cascaded down an embellished shoulder. A black and white diamondback rattler encircled the man's neck, the tail curling down his back, and balancing on the rattle a bejeweled crown.

The man looked like a magic lamp lost by a careless genie.

Even in New York, these two souls cast a spell of eerie doom. A path cleared before them, as if what they were might be contagious.

Julie stood transfixed by the spectacle until the whispering men disappeared into the crowd. They made her wonder. Did we all have pictures on our bodies? And what stories did they tell?

The ticket windows were just ahead, but she had taken only a few steps when a tall coal-black man with grizzled white hair, lean as a prophet wearing blood red drawstring sweats and a black hoodie over his head and down around his bare shoulders, wove diagonally through the crowd as if he were riding a wave. Head bobbing, a haint with burning eyes, favoring a game leg, he bore down on Julie like a smoking corpse.

In one hand held high he thumbed an old tin toy that whirled and showered sparks. Large toy rings on every finger sparkled like diamonds, emeralds, sapphires and rubies. She gulped when she saw what he waved like a flag in his other hand: a little leftover Halloween mummy, its white wrappings unraveling in the air. The man's bare chest was spectacular! Blazing with a crimson tattoo of the Sacred Heart encircled by a ring of brilliant turquoise eyes with glowing golden wings.

Striding toward her he stared into her eyes and spoke unmistakably to her alone, his voice like the sound of the ocean, as he shook the little mummy doll in her face and showered her with sparks. *"WHO WAS DEAD HAS COME BACK TO LIFE! THE TIME OF WAITING IS OVER! AWAKE I SAY! AWAKE!"*

Julie jumped out of his way, holding her breath, as she watched the dark glittering man ebb away from her.

Still moving, he turned and stared back at her thundering, *"WE ARE THE MORNING STAR! THE KINGDOM HAS COME!"*

Tattooed zombies and bejeweled prophets.

Real life was beginning to look and feel like the strangest of dreams.

"I can't hear you! Where are you?"

"Port Authority!" They had plans to have dinner tonight. She didn't want to see Ed again and was glad to have to cancel. After meeting him at the Met, and getting together for dinner twice, she wanted to back off. She couldn't say why, just that her instincts were in an uproar. Still, she felt she had to get together with him one more time to end it nicely.

"Why are you there?"

"My grandmother had a heart attack. I'm going home."

"I've been calling you for days!"

"I haven't checked my messages," she lied.

"What is your grandmother's phone number?"

"Ed, I have to go. My bus leaves in a few minutes."

"Give me your grandmother's number!"

"I'll call when I get back. I told you I have to go!" Julie ended the call.

It was a long, silent moment before Dr. Edward Henry slammed his fist down so hard electrodes jiggered across the stainless steel table. A tall beaker rolled off and hit the cement floor, the shattered glass flying.

The monkey screamed frantically.

SEVEN

APPLE PIES & 100 PENNIES

Julie's bus was pulling out of its loading dock, when she happened to glance out the window.

Dressed in black plastic trash bags, a barefoot man stood on the pavement speaking to a poster from a museum showing one of Van Gogh's self-portraits.

The man was gesturing passionately, his hands flying about like excited birds. His eyes burned like Vincent's, his mouth working strenuously.

Vincent gazed back at him with great intensity and, it seemed to Julie, with great compassion.

The bus was about half full leaving New York and Julie had the seat to herself. She leaned back, in no mood for conversation, afraid for Gran, annoyed with Ed, even more so with herself, as the bus made its way down the spiraling ramp.

Out on the highway, men were plowing snow, trucks scattering salt. Cars slid sideways on the ice, even the bus for one long terrifying minute. Snow coming down heavily.

Inside the bus, Julie felt a chill. Her heart aching with worry, tears stung her eyes.

Would Gran be all right? What if she dies before I get there?

That was unthinkable. So she took a deep breath and gazed out the window. Too bad the reason for her visit was so grim. Even so, it would be good to get out of the city. Julie loved Manhattan, but living with all the traffic, concrete, and noise got wearing after a while, especially since she had grown up near prairie and corn fields in the Midwest, and then with Gran at Norwood in woodsy Massachusetts.

Living among the striking skyscrapers and elegant brownstones, she still missed waking up to the bright pink and gold sunrises of her childhood. Her mother's garden, so lush, so filled with flowers! Roses, emperor irises, holly hocks and brown eyed susans; Jack in the pulpit, a row of peonies and lily of the valley; raspberry bushes and a rambling strawberry patch. Their home had been part of a new suburb, most of the homes less than ten years old, built on the verge of farmland.

In the shallows of a nearby pond, she had stared wide-eyed as tadpoles hatched from their jelly eggs, and watched each day as the tadpoles turned into frogs. She played in prairie, the wild grasses over her head when she was four. Black and gold garter snakes streaked across the paths, hawks glided overhead, cornfields spread out to the horizon, the Good Year blimp sailing overhead.

In New York, she often yearned for the fragrance of fresh cut grass, to hear the crickets and cicadas. She missed fireflies at dusk. Longed for a sunset and the soothing peace of twilight.

Before her father left, she'd been happy. She had a handsome father and beautiful mom. Their front and back lawn covered with morning dew gleamed as if all the stars from the night before had fallen down upon it to sleep. Granny Norwood, who she knew was a doctor, gave her a microscope for her fifth birthday and Julie set up her lab in the garage next to the rake and the grass cutter. Kneeling on old newspaper, she arranged the microscope and slides on top of an overturned cardboard box.

Spellbound, she'd peered through the eyepiece and gazed down upon the beauty and intricacy of an otherwise invisible world. She sprinkled salt and sugar crystals on slides. Explored the orderly architecture of a fragment of bee hive; the translucent beauty of a sloughed snake skin found in the prairie. Compared the bee and the ant. Admired the wings of butterflies.

In her mother's garden she turned over rocks to spy worms sliding into their holes and bugs that looked like tanks lumber away. She caught toads, then let them go. Amazed, she watched a cocoon open and release a moist butterfly. On warm summer mornings she stared in awe at the dew bejeweled webs of their garden spiders.

She'd been so happy! The world was beautiful and full of wonder. And then, one night, her mother and father quarreled, and her father disappeared into that night, forever. And Julie's world fell apart.

Julie loved New York, but suddenly felt starved for a night full of stars, and missed her grandmother so much it frightened her. Pearl sounded urgent. And that wasn't like her.

Heading north to Norwood, gazing out the bus window as the snow flew by, Julie could almost see Gran's face.

Louise Norwood, at ninety-three, with her chiseled cheek bones and white hair styled in a page-boy, had the look of an eagle in retirement. Except for her cornflower blue eyes, and her petal soft skin gathered at the corners of her smile like two small dumplings. Except, for her gentleness.

A reedy old fashioned New Englander, Louise moved slowly, a thoughtful, purposeful way about her. Patient, kindly, a somewhat reserved woman, she wore floral dresses in shades of rose or blue or violet by day; more subdued dresses for the evening in blue or grey with a pearl pin, a delicately carved ivory necklace, or a strand of jet. The combination of warm intelligence and graceful precision had made Louise Norwood a beloved baby doctor in Norwood for many years.

Julie remembered her grandfather, too, Dr. Warren Shaw, MD, much older than Gran, who died of a heart attack, or grief, about six months after his son disappeared. Even though she was only six then, she had warm memories of him.

She remembered being so little she could sit next to him on his wingback chair as he read the evening paper, smoking a cigar. Probably why she still loved a cigar's aroma. But the only thing she remembered him telling her that had really impressed her was that he had rode bareback with Indians as a boy out west. Which explained the bronze Indian on a rearing horse on the coffee table in their living room at Norwood.

Louise had kept her maiden name, having married late, and by then an established doctor.

Everywhere at Norwood, on the grand piano, along the mantle over the fireplace, arranged in clusters on walls and small end tables, there were photographs of the men of the Norwood family, many of whom had lived and died at sea. Photographs of the women, too; strong looking women, enduring women, like Gran.

Ben Norwood's unexplained disappearance was not new to Norwood. Only the unresolved mystery of what had happened to him was bewildering, and heart rending.

Gran had saved her. Without Gran, Julie was certain, she would still be lost and wandering behind that grey curtain woven by grief and anger.

She spent two years alone with her mother after her father disappeared, when she had been "almost sick," as she heard her mother tell a neighbor. Afraid of the dark and too thin, crying herself to sleep every night, missing her father. Possessed by a childhood terror without a name.

In the photo Julie kept of Gran on her bureau in New York, Gran was sitting in the garden on a lawn chair, with Dandy III, her black and white bull terrier, lying at her feet, happily worrying a hose the gardener had left about. Gran smiling, seemingly at ease, considering all her sorrows and concerns. Both her husband and daughter-in-law were dead, her son had mysteriously disappeared, and she had an eight year old granddaughter to raise. Louise then in her eighties.

Thinking of that photo, Julie felt some envy. She was never at ease. Why? She could always find a reason but which one was the real one? She sighed, tired of her sorrow and its unrelenting hold on her.

Or was she the one holding on?

Unlike most people, Julie never carried photographs of her family. Instead, she carried one of Norwood.

Because a home like Norwood, over two hundred years old, was faithful and unchanging in ways people were not.

She reached into her bag and found her wallet. Finger and thumb, searching in a little pocket, she pulled out a small black and white photo.

An old photograph, only three inches long by two inches wide, the outer edge a scalloped white border, and within that one, a border of delicate curlicues like black lace. The photo was in black and white and greys but Julie knew well the red brick home covered with ivy and the roof of terra cotta tiles.

The picture had been taken in winter. No people or cars to suggest life or motion or even the date it had been taken, only the home, the fir trees, and the lawn lightly sugared with snow.

The photograph seemed, despite the snow, a moment of arrested time, as if the house had been found asleep, like an enchanted fairy tale castle, where everyone and everything within slept.

As if, inside, the gleaming grand piano slumbered and the bronze Indian on his horse drowsed, while Pearl dreamed over a batch of dough she had begun to roll out for dinner biscuits. At the top of the spiral staircase, a black and white dog snoozed, while in their respective rooms, a grandmother dozed in her chair by the window, and a young girl napped in her room that looked out on the back garden and tossing elms. Sprawled forward at a small table, the child rested her head on her arms as she slept among hundreds of tiny puzzle pieces.

Julie held the picture as she gazed out the window of the bus as homes surrounded by leafless trees flew by.

The day after her mother's funeral, Julie and Gran flew back to Norwood where they began their new life together.

A few weeks after Julie enrolled in a nearby school, her teacher requested a conference with Louise. When they learned the story of disappearance and death, they understood the girl's lack of attention, why her performance was below expectation, and her lack of interest in playing with other children.

Julie's teacher promised to try to draw her out gently, and keep Dr. Norwood informed.

Julie had not felt like playing, and she heard nothing in class. Finally, there was too much to explain.

Where did your father go? When is he coming back? Your mother is dead?

During those first few months, while she did badly in all other subjects at school, she did excel at reading and art. She loved books and pictures, and books with pictures most of all. She would lay on the floor in the library at Norwood or sit in one of wingback chairs, turning the tissue thin pages of illustrated editions of Alice in Wonderland, The Swiss Family Robinson, Treasure Island, and several books of fairy tales.

Soon, she began to draw, copying from the illustrations. There were books about flowers and gardening, too, especially roses. And as the family had been seafaring for so long, there were several large atlases. Her father had a great interest in archaeology, so there were books that told the story of archaeological finds, ancient cities, and books of Greek and Roman myths. All these, Julie loved, and they, too, saved her.

As the months passed, her grandmother and Pearl and Dandy were the only companions she wanted. And her drawing, and Norwood's books.

Pearl was already a great friend. During Julie's summer vacations at Norwood, Pearl had taught her how to braid clover and make apple pies as big as her five year old hand.

After she finished her homework, Julie drew, stretched out on the living room floor before the fireplace. Her grandmother napped before dinner so she didn't see her until then.

Despite their great difference in age, the grieving grandmother and heartbroken granddaughter set adrift by life, yet joined by fate, became companions to one another. True, Gran was quiet and reserved. She didn't sing like Julie's mother, or swing her up in the air like her father, yet Julie remembered pleasant hours spent with her.

During long summer afternoons Julie watched her play solitaire at the dining room table. The table set for dinner, wooden blinds drawn against the mid-day heat, sunlight kissing the silver napkin rings and the crystal water glasses.

Julie stood at her side and watched as her grandmother lay out long columns of cards, the kings and queens and jacks leading, emblazoned with red hearts and diamonds, black spades and clubs, snapping each card lightly against the starched linen cloth. Her grandchild, brow furrowed, elbows on the table, mesmerized by the summer heat and by her grandmother's graceful movements, as summer flies buzzed against the screens.

Back then, Norwood was not air-conditioned, and the summers so hot Julie wanted to lie down and take a nap, but she remembered wanting the day to be whole without any dark missing patches.

Maybe she had been afraid to sleep. Afraid that she might wake and her grandmother would be gone. That she would find herself lost once more behind the grey curtain, in that place of terror.

Sometimes, after dinner, Gran would paint young Julie's badly bitten fingernails a cheerful red. Julie sitting still so as not to smudge the polish. Spreading her fingers, her hands looked like little fans, as grandmother and granddaughter, heads bent close, admired the bright red dots.

Other evenings, Julie would open a little treasure chest Gran gave her that held one hundred pennies. Julie holding each copper penny, and looking for the date, Gran patiently and painlessly taught her what seemed the impossible feat of counting from one to one hundred.

Julie sighed. Once she left Norwood for New York, there had been too few visits and not enough phone calls to Gran. But as a child she had taught herself to lose herself in books and pictures. And in New York she had done just that. No friends, except for Lorraine, just acquaintances. No lasting romance.

For the terror had pursued her there. She didn't even know where the terror came from. A therapist, she had seen for a time, asked her about those two years when life was a grey blur and she had been "almost sick." But whenever she tried to think about that time, she could remember nothing.

The snow shrouded landscape rushed by the bus window as Julie gazed down at the photo of Norwood in her hand. Nothing moved and nothing had changed. Except for a heart attack.

Where was the dragon? Was he holding this picture firmly?

EIGHT

BLACK & WRIGGLING

Despite icy roads, and worries about her grandmother, Julie had been able to sleep. Unfortunately, she had also been able to dream.

She was giving birth, but not to a child. The thing flying out of her, wet and slippery, black and all muscle. And all about it a ruffle of flesh fluttered through the air as it catapulted forward birthing itself.

Abnormally vital, it throbbed and rippled, beating its black ruffle like wings, propelling itself forward, up and out, flying forth into the world—

"Lenox! Lenox, Massachusetts!"

Startled awake, Julie staggered to her feet, grabbed her bags and disembarked, stumbling half asleep.

The cold wind stung her face as she trudged through snow a foot deep, covering everything in a brilliant glittering white, beneath a hazy full moon.

She remembered reading that more people died during a full moon. Growing up without father or mother, she had often felt quite alone, but in the back seat of the cold dark cab, hurrying home to her grandmother tonight, Julie knew she was on her way to a loneliness and isolation she had never dreamed of.

NINE

LOUISE NORWOOD

Louise Norwood knew she was dying.

She had not been a doctor all her life for nothing. This had not been her first heart attack, only the first one she had not been able to hide from Julie and Pearl.

And this time, the attack had not been minor. She had refused to go to the hospital, and her physician and good friend knew if he fought her it would only make things worse. Finally, he kissed her cheek, and left her in Pearl's care.

Louise sighed heavily. Since the attack she felt so tired! She wanted to sleep, but she could not allow herself to rest. She had a decision to make, and it was not an easy one. Which was why she had put it off so long.

Well, it didn't get much later than this.

It had also become difficult to think clearly. Short films of her life danced before her eyes like over bright reflections on water. The joy of her wedding day, the indescribable happiness the day she and Warren brought their new son Benjamin home from the adoption agency; the heartbreak and despair the night Ben disappeared. But she had to stop reminiscing! She didn't know how long she had left. She must decide!

Should she keep her long kept secret to herself? Or should Julie know the truth. Louise did not know why they never heard from Benjamin again. But she did know why he left Norwood that night in so much pain, because she was the one who caused it. And when he disappeared, overwhelmed by guilt, she'd told no one what they'd spoken of that night.

Dr. Norwood knew much about the human body and its afflictions. But when it came to those she loved, and their feelings, she often felt unsure, and had too often made the wrong decision. She knew she'd done only three things right in her life: marrying Warren, adopting Ben, and taking Julie home with her. Well, becoming a baby doctor had been wonderful, too.

But for a smart woman, as she liked to think of herself, she'd made far too many mistakes concerning her family. She had treated Ben's fevers and sore throats with confidence, but she had failed him once so profoundly, her mistake had broken all of their hearts, and she had lost her son forever.

Louise Elizabeth Norwood, at ninety-three, had lived a long life. It was only natural that she had buried many of her family, unfortunately her husband as well.

But she had not expected to lose her child. No mother would.

She did not know how she survived the grief, guilt, and anger that tore her apart every day of her life since the night he vanished. Not knowing if he would ever return. Not knowing if he was alive, or dead.

As a boy, Ben had not cared much for school but spent hours practicing magic tricks, looked forward to the week's episode of *Twilight Zone*, read the books he loved, especially books about Egypt, and dinosaurs, and outer space. From spare lumber a local carpenter had given him, he'd built himself a wonderful two-story tree house. He taught himself to play the piano. Everything from Bach to Boogie-Woogie, and any and all popular songs. Her son had many talents but he had not settled on his life's work, even after marriage and the birth of his child. Instead, he continued his extensive reading, and drove a bus.

Louise suggested he become a doctor. He had his inheritance, so supporting himself and his family during medical school would not be an obstacle. But he never expressed interest.

That night, the last time Louise saw him, he'd called ahead to say he wanted to stay at Norwood for a few days. He and Catherine had argued again and it was possible they might divorce.

Unfortunately, that evening, Louise could not resist bringing up the old subject of his work. Whether he and Catherine divorced or not, had he decided what he wanted to do with his life? He had a young child to think about. And why was he still driving a bus, when his inheritance made that unnecessary?

She had pushed too hard, but as usual he tried to make a joke of it, batting her arguments away gently. "Mother, you love medicine. But it's not for me." Smiling broadly, he added, "I just didn't get that gene."

A small gust of breath had escaped her. "Of course you didn't," she had said quietly. And then she finally told him he was adopted. They had always planned to tell him, but kept putting it off, never finding the right moment.

"You're not my mother?"

How that hurt. It still did.

Then, "Who are my parents?"

Louise was a doctor so she knew the heart could not turn to stone and then lodge in your throat, but in that moment that's exactly how it felt. "I don't know. We didn't want to know. You were ours. We were so happy to have found you."

"You never told me."

"Ben, you're still my son!"

He stumbled up from the table, shaking his head. "I don't know who I am." He grabbed his jacket and rushed out the front door. Drove away and disappeared from their lives forever. Neither Catherine nor Louise nor Julie heard from him again.

That he'd left angry and confused had been her fault. But why abandon his wife and child? It had never made sense. Still, Louise never told either Catherine or Julie what had made him storm off that night. Should she tell Julie now? How would that help her?

After his disappearance, she called hospitals in every state. Police departments. Placed ads in newspapers. But she never learned what happened to him. Six months later, Warren died of a heart attack, or grief.

Telling Julie now why Ben left that night would do no good and might cause harm, for Louise feared Julie might look at her with that same lost look and say, *"You're not my grandmother?"*

No. She would not risk losing Julie. Not even on her death bed.

Over the years, Louise missed Ben terribly. But his leaving, and Catherine's early death, had brought Julie to her, the unexpected joy late in her life.

After Ben's disappearance, during Julie's increasingly frequent visits, while still living with her mother, the child seemed distant and detached. No longer gay and full of life. She would abandon her dolls, leave puzzles incomplete. Her microscope gathered dust. She grew pale and thin.

"What do I do now?" she'd chanted, pacing Norwood utterly lost—until she began to draw. The troubling thing was she would draw for hours. Really, until she was stopped. It was obsessive, but the child had lost the father she adored under mysterious circumstances.

Two years later, when Catherine died, Louise remembered how happy she was to bring Julie home to Norwood. They would both start over. Julie was eight then. Louise, eighty-two.

Without a second thought, she sold her practice and retired without a single regret, wanting to spend time with Julie. How she had wished she was younger and had more energy!

"Oh, Benjamin," Louise sighed with a bittersweet smile. "How you would love your daughter!"

As a child, he'd been so earnest and charming and mischievous. Soft freckles over his handsome nose. His brown eyes, serious yet gentle. A quick smile, easy going, yet determined. The boy had grown to be a warm handsome man.

Louise clutched the coverlet. What had become of him? Terrible enough to lose a child before one's own time. But not to know?

Louise checked her pulse with trembling fingers. She had observed the onset and procedure of death far too often to mistake it for anything less. Now, with some fear, and curiosity, she awaited her own.

But she was troubled for Julie. True, it was another era. Quite different from her own. But wasn't love still the most important thing? And Julie had not found her love. She loved painting, and it was an enormous gift to find the work one loved. But as her grandmother, Louise wanted Julie to have love, too.

She could not insure her granddaughter's happiness, but she was in a position to help.

To that effect, her will was in order. Julie would inherit Norwood and a modest estate. That would surprise her, as she may have assumed Norwood would be left to the Seaman's Institute.

But Louise had changed her will when she realized how seriously Julie painted. She would need financial security to give her the freedom to develop this gift, or another she might choose later. After all, Van Gogh, Cassatt, and Monet, to name only a few, had all been supported by family money. One wondered how far they would have gotten without it.

How many talents were crushed by financial burdens? How many never had a chance? She would not let that happen to her granddaughter.

Although offered help by Louise (something of a test, those offers were), Julie had insisted on supporting herself. Having proven her mettle, she would not have to work a job.

For, in addition to Norwood, Julie would inherit a fine bit of money. More than she could have imagined. The family's wealth was not obvious but preserved soundly. Her seafaring forefathers had lived short lives on dangerous seas yet resisted the temptation to live for today only. Their prudent wives helped them save as the family's importing company grew and prospered from one generation to another.

Louise had provided for her granddaughter. She had done the best she could. Everything was finally in place.

Except one last thing.

A most unusual and unexpected gift.

TEN

INHERITANCE

The delicate frost forest etching the cab's window framed Julie's view of Norwood, bringing her treasured photograph to life as if by magic.

The stately Georgian home stood in the snow storm, lamps softly glowing on either side of the door promising welcome and sanctuary.

Yet, Julie knew that just inside that promising door crouched memories that never tired of rearing up and savaging her heart.

Beneath the snowy mantle, Norwood had suffered years of neglect. Inside, Pearl kept the home beautifully clean and polished, but Norwood's grounds had long gone unattended.

Gran's grief, with a logic of its own, had moved her to dismiss the gardener. Her home would mirror her mourning.

Massive fir trees and brawny elms embraced the house of grief. Evergreen bushes grew wildly encroaching upon the once sedate lawn, long gone to tall grass, now blanketed by snow. Untended ivy covered the house, nearly blinding the windowpanes.

Julie remembered playing in the garden when she was three and four and five. The garden so lovely then.

Goldfish swam beneath the dark olive green surface of the pond, glinting gold with black, carmine, and silver speckles. Translucent fins undulating like veils. So tame, she fed them by hand. In summer, the small pond became a verdant tangle of rosemary and watercress, thick with jack-in-the-pulpit, the air perfumed with lily of the valley.

After her father's disappearance, Julie's mother sent her to Norwood to spend that first grief stricken summer with Gran. In the heat of endless afternoons, in the shade of the old elms, Julie had lain at the side of the pond trailing her fingers among the lily pads and reeds, aching for her father's return, reciting the multiplication tables he had taught her, as if they alone were magic enough to bring him back home again.

Inside Norwood, the silver shone, the crystal water glasses sparkled, but the piano began to drift out of tune. Like a fairy tale, the Prince had gone out into the world, never to return, and his castle began to fall into ruin. Ever after, his spellbound Princess wrote letters to him, in a kind of sleep, when she was 'almost sick.'

Sick with terror

Writing to her father, once begun, became a ritual Julie relied on to keep the terror at bay. How many had she written? There were boxes in back of both closets in New York. Recent ones filled a trunk she used as an end table. Hundreds of letters. Written to her father and no where to send them. But it had helped to write them. It still did.

But why did she feel so abandoned right now when Norwood looked so beautiful in the snowy moonlight?

The cab had rumbled away into the night, tires spinning and whining as they dug into the snow and slid on the ice. Cold, as she stood in windblown snowdrifts nearly to her knees, Julie gazed up at Norwood for a few more moments. And then it all came back to her.

A Christmas visit long ago, when Julie and her mother and father, had all come to visit Gran together. When the house must have looked just like this. Radiant with snow in the lamplight.

Once upon a time, when they were a family.

So long ago.

After all these years, how intensely she still missed him. The love and the sorrow still so raw. He'd vanished, yet she thought of him so often he was always with her. Like a ghost.

As Lorraine pointed out too often, she loved a father she barely knew.

So be it.

Her father had taken her to the circus once and she'd been stunned by the courage of the brave trapeze artists reaching out to each other as they swung through the air.

When they finally grasped each other's wrist, the crowd moaned with relief and sighed for the beauty of common knowledge—we must hold on to each other, or we all fall down, plunging into a pit so deep and dark and endless, we begin to understand the meaning of Hell.

When she pretended to be asleep that night, when her father drove away and never returned, they each had let the other go. He, disappearing into thin air, leaving his daughter hovering miraculously in that same thin air, waiting for his return, and she would wait, it seemed, forever.

In a state of suspension, she could not remember the magic word that would bring him back, could not remember what she had done wrong. There was so much she could not remember. She still wondered what she might apologize for, what she could do to bring her father home.

Maybe nothing. Maybe he's dead.

The thought like an arrow pierced her heart.

Julie stood frozen in place before Norwood, unable to bear the thought of losing Gran, too. But how could she fight death?

The icy wind blew the snow about stinging her face. Her hands and feet were already numb with cold.

Just now, the desire to sink down into the soft white snow and let it slowly bury her felt nearly overpowering. She would embrace this thing that was clawing at her grandmother. Let death take her, too. Why not? What did she have to live for?

She remembered the nightmare she had on the bus. Her birthing a monstrous thing. *Not now.* Gran needed her.

She let herself in through the low iron gate. Trudged through the snow and up the few steps leading to the door, where she rang the bell. A few minutes later, she heard the lock drawn. The door opened wide.

"Child! Come in out of that cold!"

Julie had never been so grateful to see Pearl. She really needed one of the old housekeeper's hugs she happily got lost in as a child.

Pearl and Julie hugged each other tight.

"How is she?"

"I do believe she might pass, Jewelee." Pearl called her by the pet name known only by the two of them. The two women looked at each other, their eyes brimming with tears.

"I'll go up now."

Julie ran up the stairs, and when she got to the top, took a deep breath before she walked down the hall toward Gran's room. On the way, she glanced at the closed door to her father's room.

Something like Miss Haversham, Louise Norwood preserved her son's room just as he left it on his wedding day, for a marriage she did not approve. Pearl had her orders. She was to clean the room, which was quite unlike Miss Haversham, but she was not to move a thing. And she hadn't, all these years.

Julie had never been able to enter his room after he disappeared.

my fault, my fault

The child within chanting her guilt like a nightmare jump rope song, she hurried down the hall to Gran.

About to enter Gran's room she heard the old phonograph player quietly playing one of Gran's opera records. She'd only learned recently from Pearl, that Gran's earliest ambition had been to be an opera singer but she eventually had gotten interested in medicine and become a doctor. Julie had grown up at Norwood accompanied by the sound of opera coming from whatever room Gran occupied. Mainly her office where she caught up on her medical and insurance forms for her patients.

Dandy III, Gran's black and white Boston Terrier, looked up from his post at the side of her bed and whimpered. He knew.

Julie patted his head and scratched his chin, as he licked her hand in greeting, but he was inconsolable.

"Gran?" Julie whispered. "Are you awake?"

Louise Norwood slowly opened her eyes, and seeing her granddaughter, smiled. "Julie dear."

Julie sat on a nearby chair to take her grandmother's hand in hers. "How do you feel?"

"Tired. I keep wanting to sleep."

"Are you in pain?"

"Only with the onset of the attack. How are you?"

"I'm fine. Want me to stay with you a while?"

"No, I want to sleep a bit. Pearl can give you something to eat. You must be hungry."

"I'm starving!" That was a lie, but Julie was glad to see another small smile on her grandmother's face. In their small household, Julie's appetite was legendary.

"Have dinner. I'll rest a bit. Come back later."

"Of course."

"I have a gift for you. And you will never guess what it is!"

"Oh?" Julie kissed her gently on the cheek. Smiling, Gran's eyes had already closed.

Julie stared down at her for a moment, then left the room, full of fear.

In her own room, she found her backpack unpacked and her bath drawn, fragrant with scented oils that promised to soothe her mind and body.

Pearl, kind Pearl.

Undressing quickly, she slipped into the inviting bath and as her muscles unclenched, she couldn't stop the tears.

Gran's heart attack unleashed all her old fears and sorrows. Allowed the terror to take a giant leap forward, with only that grey curtain of merciful forgetfulness to protect her.

Unconsciously she drew her knees up, wrapped her arms around them and rested her head on them.

If she pretended to be asleep, if she held her breath and did not move a muscle, if she played dead, would death pass Gran by?

But hadn't she been playing dead for some time? No thought of a future marriage or children, no direction in her work. Her life a perfect record of absence and loss and silence.

Painting was silent. Like watching her grandmother play solitaire, and fishing with her father. Like copying Greek myths, as she'd done as a child, into a spiral notebook with a quill pen. Watching the sun set and twilight emerge. Stroking the golden fish. Her life, a portrait in silence.

She would not tell, she could not tell, not even herself, what crouched behind the grey curtain.

Maybe it was the comforting warmth and pleasing fragrance of the apricot scented bath oil that led her gently, and unexpectedly, to a pleasant memory of a favorite child-hood ritual.

Remembering, she smiled and wiped away her tears. Shortly after she came to live at Norwood, Gran gave her a tin box filled with jewelry she no longer wore.

Awake at dawn, and standing before her mirror in her pajamas, Julie would cover herself with Gran's vermilion coral and carved ivory necklaces, a filigreed silver pin and jet beads, ropes of pearls, a glittering tiara, a topaz brooch, and a sapphire ring that swung on her small fingers. Turning before the mirror, the morning light shot through the faceted stones and flew about the walls of her room, rainbows of light dappling the faces of her entranced dolls.

Bejeweled and carrying an ivory fan, she would slowly descend the carpeted staircase long before Pearl arrived and Gran woke.

The little girl pacing solemn as a priestess reaching out and giving each favored object a light pat, for there was magic purpose to this ceremony.

Circling the piano, passing before the fireplace, reaching out to pat the bronze Indian on horseback in the living room; walking around the dining room table her ringed hand glittering, braceleted arms outstretched as she spun in circles in the library.

Only then, would she return, at the same slow measured pace, climbing the spiral staircase through the early morning light, the jewelry her ballast, tying her firmly to the grandmother who loved her, as she made certain, once more, that home had survived the night; not disappearing like her mother and father.

Only then, would she return to her sunny room, return the magical jewels to their box, and work on a puzzle until Pearl called her and Gran to breakfast striking three tones on a small xylophone hung on the dining room wall.

The fragrant bath water so soothing, Julie closed her eyes and smiled again. All these years later, she sometimes wore three necklaces.

Feeling much better after her bath and a quick dinner with Pearl in the kitchen, Julie wanted to give Gran another 15 minutes before she went up to see her. She would have had an hour and a half nap by then.

To pass the time, Julie visited Norwood's library, her favorite room, where she had finally learned to read, stumbling over the words and sentences, wondering if it would ever be easy, as Gran and Pearl listened and assured her.

And when that moment finally arrived it felt like magic! The words springing to life, leaping and running after each other and she could keep up! Eager and fascinated and delighted by the story unfolding before her.

After that, Gran and Pearl had a hard time getting her to leave the library at bedtime. Books were like living things to her. So many stories pulsing with life, just waiting for her inside those books!

So over the years, she spent many wonderful happy hours in the library reading. And tonight, Pearl had laid and lit a fire for her, knowing Julie would stop in. The fragrance of burning logs and the warmth and beauty of the fire filled the room.

The ceilings were twice the height of those in the rest of the house, the walls lined with bookcases; a narrow spiraling heavily carved and polished wood staircase led to a second tier of books and a walkway that encircled the room.

By day, sunlight poured through an arched window of leaded glass that filled one entire wall framed by dark green velvet drapes, held back by silken tassels, and hung from brass rods to the floor.

Tonight, several brass candlestick lamps under broad black shades cast pools of golden light. In front of the fireplace, the large comfortable leather couch and the wing back chair and hassock covered in a worn French blue damask looked inviting as usual. The floor carpeted with a pale cream rug with several oriental throws scattered about.

Julie had always loved the moss green Persian prayer rug with violet designs, the bold Hamadan woven in black, tangerine, and turquoise devices, and a lovely Bukhara in shades of dusty rose and midnight blue.

But where was her favorite?

Each time Pearl vacuumed the library she arranged the oriental rugs according to her liking that particular morning, so now, Julie had to look around for the one she loved most.

"Ah, ha!" There it was at the foot of the spiral staircase. She walked over and sat down on the second step to admire "her" rug. This was the rug she chose to play on as a toddler.

Looking at it now, she thought, and not for the first time, how incongruous it was for this room. Or for the house, for that matter. The rug depicted a pair of tigers striding through a jungle, interwoven with shining threads of gold, with heavy black outlines around the tigers and trees.

Julie smiled remembering how she lay on the tigers' backs, trying to pull their tails, happily curling up with them and falling asleep, as if she were one of their cubs.

How had this rug found a place in her grandparents' otherwise comfortable yet conservative home? And why had it held such a place of honor, all these years, right along with their collection of antique rugs?

She had never thought to ask before, and now, it might be too late. A little family mystery reminding her of the larger one. Julie stood up and began to climb the staircase, seeing nothing.

She had no words for what she felt about her father's disappearance, only a well of infinite darkness inside her that she could, only sometimes, recognize as sorrow. Sorrow, but never anger. She could never get to the anger. Being here at Norwood only brought memories back. And maybe that was why she had spent so little time here since she moved to New York.

The clock on the mantle began chiming half-past seven. Time to look in on Gran and relieve Pearl.

And wondering what sort of gift Gran had for her!

"Is she sleeping?"

Pearl nodded and got up. They went out into the hall.

"I can sit with her now. Get some sleep."

"Ah will, but ah'll be back 'bout two. Then you can get some sleep. I don't need much these days anyhow. When you ole, you don't need much. The young need their sleep."

Julie grinned. Pearl still thought of her as a child. But Pearl must be in her eighties now. "Okay, Pearl. Thanks."

"Don't thank me or ah'm goin' to get mad," she said with a fierce face, then smiled, kissed Julie on the forehead, patted her head, and walked down the hall to her room, kept for the times she occasionally stayed over.

Julie walked back inside Gran's room, happy to see her awake.

"Did you have something to eat, dear?"

"Yes, Gran. How are you feeling?" Julie pulled a chair closer to the bed and sat down.

"Much better now that I've had that little nap."

"Good!" And she did look better. Color in her cheeks, even a little light in her eyes. Maybe she would recover after all. A warm hope flickered in Julie's heart.

"I've been thinking of your father."

"I think of him, a lot," Julie murmured.

"We all suffered so much. And, I feel, I failed him."

"No you didn't!"

"We mean well, but we all fail each other in some way."

Julie reached out for her grandmother's hand. "You never failed me."

"Then I've done something right." But too much wrong.

A tear slipped down Julie's cheek. "Don't go."

Louise took a deep breath as if savoring it. "It's my time, dear. And I am curious. I wonder if I'll see Warren again. But before I go—"

"Yes?" Glad to see her grandmother smile, Julie hoped she was changing the subject or she would soon be crying uncontrollably.

"I told you I have a gift for you."

"Save it for Christmas," Julie shot back.

Louise shook her head and smiled. "I think I better give it to you now."

"What is it?"

"Do you see that box on the table?"

Julie retrieved it. And now she was very curious.

A lovely wooden box. Beautifully hand carved, old, but in good condition. Two drawers above the substantial base. And the carving exquisite. The entire cover and all four sides were deeply carved into roses and vines with the barest touch of paint and gilt still clinging to the wood. In the lamp light, the traces of gold glittered.

Julie laughed she was so delighted. "It's beautiful!" And when she tilted the box, something inside slid to the back.

Louise smiled. "The rosewood box is beautiful, but the gift is inside."

Julie noticed the finely wrought brass lock, but no key. And when she tried to lift the lid, she found the box locked.

"Here you are." Louise reached for a key on a long silver chain on her bedside table. "Take the key, but open it later, I'd like to tell you something about your gift first."

Louise smiled contentedly, relishing her surprise.

"My grandmother gave it to me, and it was given to her by her grandmother. In fact," Louise paused for breath and closed her eyes for a moment, then opened them and continued, "it has been in the family, passed down from grandmother to granddaughter, since the 1850's, when the family acquired it. Now it's yours."

Louise patted Julie's hand smiling. "You'll never guess what it is." Julie had been tracing the carving with her fingers. Now she looked up at Gran.

"The box holds a literary collector's item I've always thought, of all those who inherited it, you would appreciate it most. You love to read so much, and also because of your love of old things. I remember how you cherished the sampler we found at a roadside stand that summer in Vermont. You were about eleven then." Louise closed her eyes and smiled.

Worried about tiring her grandmother, Julie sat back, curious, but prepared to wait, or learn more tomorrow.

But Louise took a deep breath, opened her eyes, and rallied.

"Inside the box is the original manuscript of Mary Shelley's *Frankenstein,* written in her own hand."

Julie blinked. "What?"

"It's worth something, my dear, probably a great deal. I've never read the manuscript, but we all know the story," she said, smiling at her granddaughter expectantly.

"That's wonderful, Gran," Julie managed. "You think it's authentic?" Couldn't be. Could it?

"Oh yes, dear, I'm quite certain."

"But how? How would you know for sure?"

"The family was already in shipping in 1850, when Nathan Norwood's son, Jeremy, bought the box with the manuscript inside from a collector fallen on hard times in London." Louise closed her eyes. She looked quite comfortable, as if she were about to fall asleep. Julie stood up, ready to tiptoe out of the room.

"Julie?" the old woman murmured.

"Gran, please rest. We'll talk tomorrow."

"It's yours now, it's all yours," she said, in barely a whisper.

Julie kissed her on the cheek. "I love you, Gran."

"I love you, my dear," Gran whispered, as she closed her eyes with a smile on her lips and drifted off to sleep.

Julie lay in the dark, afraid of the dark, trying to fall asleep but not wanting to.

She did not like seeing someone she loved slip into sleep so easily with death so near, reminding her that there was no question of fighting and winning. No one and nothing was hers for keeps. All that she owned was this fleeting moment.

For she could not help feeling, no matter how much better Gran looked, that Death was prowling about their home tonight, and Death was in a hungry mood.

ELEVEN

LITTLE DEATH DOLLS

The morning after Gran's funeral, Julie caught the first bus back to New York, then a cab straight to her loft.

She only knew one way to deal with her grief. She needed to be alone, and she needed to work.

Slipping the key into the lock, she opened the door to the loft, dropped her bags on the floor, punched in the code to disarm the alarm system, grateful for the dusty quiet. It was Sunday. The street beneath her windows deserted and still.

Ever since she watched her grandmother's casket lowered into the ground, she felt numb. Her mouth full of dry sticks. Life had come to a full dark dead stop. Like her father leaving, and her mother dying, all over again. Every thought and feeling she bumped into felt sharp and hurt.

After the funeral, she found herself alone at an unmarked border. Ahead, there seemed nowhere to go, and she knew there was no going back.

She had once read, "We live and die alone in separate cities." But she couldn't remember who to hate for it.

Even after the funeral she couldn't believe Gran was gone. And every time she remembered, it hit her like a train.

She came to the loft to solve her sorrow, but which one?

Princess! I've got something for you. Pick a hand—Any hand!

The first hand she chose would be empty. The second always held a bar of chocolate.

Her mother and father, hadn't they both seemed too good to be true? Her dad, handsome with a smile like Gregory Peck's. And her mom, so beautiful she really belonged in a 1940's movie dressed in chiffon.

Julie remembered a birthday cake her mother made for her one year—six layers and each a different color. Mom waking her each morning singing *"You are my sunshine, my only sunshine . . . "* But after her father left, the cakes were store bought, and the house became terribly silent. And now Gran, gone too.

Julie wondered if she had somehow always known that her father would leave and her mother would die soon after. Maybe, she thought, we were all born knowing just what was going to happen and how it was going to work out. Maybe we forget on purpose. And maybe, it was the burden of forgetting certain things that made us so sad sometimes, and so very tired.

She threw the dead bolt, pulled off her coat, desperate to kill the pain.

Changing into her painting clothes, she wondered at the scary coincidence of the small mummy figures she had begun to make just a few weeks before Gran died.

Death whispering, *Just to let you know, I will be calling.*

Maybe even bringing on Gran's death?

That, of course, was totally crazy thinking!

But why was it our craziest thoughts were the ones that felt most true?

Don't think!

That's one way to deal with reality.

One that seemed like a very good idea right now.

She had cried so much the last few days. She would force her attention back to her work, over and over, if she had to.

Actually, it had been more than a year since she first felt the desire to paint a mummy. One summer, when she was nine years old, she spent a week curled up on the couch in the library at Norwood, completely enthralled, reading about the excavation of King Tut's tomb.

And ever since, she loved ancient Egyptian art and artifacts, still, mummies seemed like such a strange thing for her to paint, she had put the inspiration aside. But it kept haunting her. It wouldn't leave her alone.

Oscar Wilde once said, the best way to rid yourself of temptation was to give into it. Well, not always. After the first mummy drawing, her need to draw another little dead lady lost in time had only grown stronger.

In July, the day she signed the lease for the loft, she sat right down and drew six mummies in line and transparent washes of gold, sepia, and black inks. Then she began to paint one in oils.

She thought they might be about a new beginning.

Turning down design projects, she painted every day and as long into the night as her burning neck and shoulder muscles would allow. She rubbed on Tiger Balm. Took aspirin. The canvas was five by six feet. The largest she'd ever done.

She named it *Target Practice.* Two large mummies, nearly five feet tall. One black, one gold. Painted with white circles strategically placed on the mummies. What had she been doing?

Trying to kill Death? Then why two mummies?

The loft lit by two spotlights and a few candles, she'd painted long into the nights. Dipped a brush in turpentine, to pull away the topmost layer of paint between each strip of the wrappings she had just painted, leaving a mist of the thinnest transparent glaze of color.

The mummy's wrappings seemed to float on the glowing surface, a translucent pearl grey between those of the black wrappings; a sheer golden inlay between those of the gold.

The paint still wet she'd taken a cloth and beaten the mummies. Lashing out at the wet canvas in the middle of the night, beating up on the mummies, had she been beating up on death?

She knew she wanted them to look as if they had been whipped by centuries of wind in an eternal desert.

But the drawings and the painting had not been enough to satisfy her raw compelling need to touch one. Hold one.

So, she began making her little death dolls. Only two so far.

And she had actually taken quite a liking to Ed's name for them, although she wouldn't tolerate him or Lorraine calling them that.

To start, she bought a jointed wooden model sold in art stores for students learning to draw the human body. She had chosen a female model, twelve inches high.

Julie shivered. It was cold in the loft. A light snow still falling. She switched on one of the heaters, pulled her paint spattered grey sweatshirt over a black cotton turtleneck, and made some tea to warm up.

Neither Ed nor Lorraine liked the mummies. Why was she was so obsessed with something that gave most people the creeps?

Glancing up she smiled at "Sleeping Beauty", her first mummy figure hanging on the wall: the mummy wrapped in gauze tinted brown with tea, sealed with shellac to a rich sepia color. Attached to an eleven by fourteen inch sheet of masonite covered with canvas painted with raw umber. And finally, she'd ripped pieces of black roofing paper she'd found on the street and glued them over the mummy, not entirely covering her.

The second mummy hanging next to "Sleeping Beauty," she called "Profound Seal," wrapped and tinted similarly, attached to masonite in the same way but then she'd attached a piece of old window screen she'd found on the street, covering the mummy but leaving the feet exposed, vulnerable.

In a way, they were embarrassing. Too revealing. Wrapped, buried, bound, sealed, they were her. The stifled life. Again, self-portraits. *Christ.*

Trying to ignore her constant self doubt, needing to get started, she pulled the stool closer to the work table and sat down. Shoved the jars of brushes aside, pushed tubes of paint out of the way. Pulled a bundle of cotton gauze to her and unfolded it. Began cutting it into one inch strips. Then pulled the new wooden model out of the box and began wrapping a strip of gauze around the doll's feet.

The real surprise was how it made her feel while making them. They felt real. Even, alive. Definitely weird. Why was she making them?

Today, if nothing else, to distract her from missing Gran.

There was no denying the influence of the ancient Egyptian mummy, but she had already learned online, that mummification had been practiced, or naturally occurred, all over the planet.

In the Andes Mountains of Peru, Pre-Inca cultures mummified their rulers and placed them in caves that protected them from the moist climate.

Incredibly well-preserved bodies have been found in bogs throughout northern Britain and Scandinavia, so well preserved by the tannic acid in bog water, it was assumed they were recent murder victims. But carbon dating proved they were two thousand years old.

Okay, legs bound. Now the hips.

In Palermo, Italy, in the Cave of the Capuchins, the bodies of monks were found preserved by the climate alone.

Naturally mummified bodies of Native Americans have been found in caves in Kentucky and Tennessee. Eskimo burials were simply preserved by the extreme cold.

Even so, no other people on earth had so elaborately embalmed their dead as the Chinese of the Han Dynasty and, especially so, the Egyptians.

Before the Egyptians converted to Christianity, she'd learned they had mummified their dead for twenty-five centuries!

Now, she wrapped the strip of gauze across the small bumps that were the breasts and around the figure's small shoulders.

Her little death dolls. Maybe they frightened Ed and Lorraine. Julie knew they frightened her a little. But she had a fierce affection and protective feeling for them too.

There. She reached for her scissors and snipped the ends of the gauze knotted behind the dolls head.

The small female figure lay in her hands completely wrapped in white gauze. Like a bandage?

And was the face beneath these wrappings now riddled with white cracks, her eyes glowing white ovals, her young mouth open in a scream? A young screaming dead girl buried alive?

Art is a burning mirror.

How much did she want to see? How much did she want to feel?

She looked down at the mummy in her hands.

Well, if this was a self-portrait, apparently not much.

Julie laid the wrapped figure on the table. Reached for the can of shellac, but first dipped the brush in the dregs of her tea and tinted the wrappings a pale sepia. She dried it fast with a hair dryer hanging from a nail pounded into the table's edge. Then pried the can of shellac open. Dipped the brush in and began to soak the gauze in the sealant that would harden the gauze like armor.

Bending down close to the mummy, filling the brush and emptying it, soaking the bandages, over and over, she would seal every fold, bind every strip of wrapping.

She would make her safe.

The tears came in a rush.

Furious with Death, the mummy in one hand, she shoved tubes of paint and the glass jar full of brushes off the table, crashing to the floor.

Someday she would die. But she wanted to live first! And somehow she knew she wasn't even half awake. And that this sleep she called her life was a living death!

Laying her head down on one arm on the splintery table, the little mummy clutched in her other hand, she wept for the little dead girl inside her, bound, blinded, and gagged. The one who could not see behind the grey curtain. The one who could not tell Ed to get lost. The one who said yes to him in the first place.

Apart from her grandmother, Julie mourned a little girl living in terror of the thing that owned her, and still lurked behind that grey curtain of forgetfulness, lying in wait for what was left of her.

Wanting to eat her all up.

Sitting up and staring into the white plastic drapes, seeing nothing seemed just right.

She couldn't work anymore today. She had some free-lance work, but not until next week.

She looked around her, at the tubes of paint, brushes, and broken glass all over the floor. She would clean up this mess. Then call Ed. And get that over with.

"You're back."

"A couple of hours ago."

"You didn't call me!"

"Ed," she began with forced patience, "my grandmother died the morning after I got there. I had to arrange the funeral. I did call and left that message telling you what happened. I didn't get a chance to call again."

There was a strained silence. Time for Ed to say something comforting. He didn't.

"Where are you?"

"I'm at my loft. And I'm sorry if you were worried." *Why was she always apologizing?* And she doubted it was worry he was feeling, but she'd give him the benefit of the doubt.

And why do that?

"It's a matter of priorities, Julie. I expect you to call, to keep me informed."

Her instincts were screaming! She wanted this to be over! Why couldn't she just say that?

She picked up a strip of gauze and wrapped her thumb.

"I'll come down there."

"No." She wrapped each finger carefully.

"You like being alone!"

All four fingers were wrapped together. "Sometimes."

"You don't need anyone, do you?"

Not true. But she didn't feel up to an argument. If she did, she would have told him she never wanted to see him again. "I don't feel like talking now. I just wanted to return your call."

"Are you painting?"

"No." She wrapped her hand down to the wrist, working the gauze up along her arm.

"So you're sitting there doing nothing in that squalid, rat infested building."

"No, I did some work."

"Making more of your little death dolls?"

Julie startled, suddenly seeing her wrapped arm. "Actually, I was working on one."

"You know what I think of them."

"Yes, I do." She held her hand away from her staring at it.

"They're morbid, Julie. They're sick!"

"You're entitled to your opinion."

"I want to see you."

"I need some time alone."

"No you don't."

Julie's mummified hand clenched into a fist and pounded her thigh. "Yes—I—do!" She ended the call.

The loft was stone quiet. A memory rose to the surface of her mind like a bubble from the mouth of one of her grandmother's gold fish, rising to the surface of the pond.

Inside the transparent sphere of memory, she remembered a trip taken long ago to New York with her father. They were in the Metropolitan Museum of Art, in the Egyptian wing, where her father held her hand as they both gazed at the mummies.

That day had always been one of her few treasured memories of her father, but now, furious with Ed, seeing what she had just done, she tore at her bandaged hand and arm, ripped the wrappings off, grabbed her bag, and slammed out of the loft.

PART TWO

We must assume our existence
as broadly as we in any way can.
Everything, even the unheard of,
must be possible. . . .
Letters To A Young Poet
Rainer Maria Rilke

TWELVE

O'CONNOR

The phone had been ringing all day, and when it wasn't, Lorraine O'Connor was punching in calls. One right after the other.

Arranging for the panel discussion and the trip, she came in on a Sunday because tomorrow she would be busy finishing up on two jobs she still had in house.

Her passport and plane ticket were tucked in her red leather carry-on at home, but she still hadn't finished packing! No small concern for a textile designer fashionista. And there were a million loose ends to take care of right here at the office before she could leave for Florence on Friday.

She could not wait! Four whole days with nothing to do but talk shop with other designers.

Of course, she was going to miss Max. They were rarely apart. Only when he played out of town or during one of her occasional business trips, but it was only four days.

After three years of marriage, Lorraine still could not believe her good fortune. From the first time she saw him, a stocky guy with dirty blond hair, hunched over his alto sax in that smoke filled club—it was over. And the beauty of it was, she grinned, he still seemed to crave and adore this short, buxom, energetic red head he'd married.

In her professional life, Lorraine knew she would need to work for someone who understood the obsessed and hopelessly compulsive, but she never found the right company. So, after a few years on staff, and then some freelancing, she started her own company, O'Connor Design.

Lorraine's drawing table was a mess, and she surveyed it with a sigh of deep satisfaction. Thank God she would never again have to suit her mother's idea of order. Two walls of the studio were covered with swatches of fabric, photos, and watercolor sketches of designs.

She loved her work, and even though clients and deadlines drove her nuts she was one happy lady.

If only Max would stop with wanting to be a daddy, yesterday!

Okay, so she was pushing twenty-six, and it had taken until now to learn what she needed to know to design, polish her talent, and start her own business. She was supposed to stop now to have a baby? She was just getting started here! Sure, she wanted a baby—a couple! But this was not the right time! They were young!

Later would be better. Later, when? She didn't know. Just not now! Because right now, she couldn't wait to get to Florence!

Usually her fingers were splotched with a rainbow of colors from the markers and water colors she used to sketch her designs. An interesting effect, since she always had a fire engine red manicure. She would tell you she was a 'more is more' person. But most people got that, right away.

Lorraine loved her computer, but for getting the idea down the first time she loved to play around with markers, brushes and inks, and she was not above lipstick or shoe polish if it was the color she was after.

Everything was source material! Photography and drawings of animals from Dürer to Alice in Wonderland, of birds and butterflies, leaves and trees and flowers! Comic books, Nasa's latest shots, books on lace and crochet, antique rugs, and Japanese tattoos!

On her side table there were several books on the art of tribal people because of her talk. She was leaving for Florence in a few days to lead a panel discussion at The Annual International Convention of Textile Designers. The topic for her panel was "Pattern—An Ancient Language," and her idea. Making sure the five other designers on her panel were ready had been no small nightmare. And she still had final editing to do on her own paper. Before Saturday! A lot of work, but so much fun!

Oh, and she had to call Julie. She made a quick note, and smiled remembering meeting Julie for the first time.

Julie was straight out of college and new to the city, studying painting at the Art Student's League and working as an apprentice at a design studio. Lorraine, a few years older and a native New Yorker, had just launched her own company.

They met at the main branch of the New York Public Library in the image file department. Sitting next to each other, they fell into an easy conversation and exchanged phone numbers.

Right away, they liked each other and regarded the other's work with respect and interest so many dinners later there was no end to talk, arguments, and laughter.

Never mind that Lorraine's love for clothes was second only to her love for Max, and Julie always wore artist's black. And while marriage to Max had been the best thing that ever happened to Lorraine, Julie swore she would never marry. Never mind. They had a meeting of minds, appreciated each other's brand of humor, and liked each other's cooking. They both treasured the friendship.

The damn phone was ringing again! How was she ever going to get everything done in time to leave on Friday?

While it was annoying, Lorraine remembered those first two years when O'Connor Design was located in one corner of their one bedroom, and she'd prayed for the phone to ring.

Today, her company was doing just fine, in a two room suite on Madison Avenue in the Thirties, and she and Max had a larger apartment on the Upper West Side they were hoping to buy.

She reached for the ringing phone, deciding the next one would go to voice mail. Today was Sunday and she was leaving Friday. There were uncompleted jobs in house, her paper needed a final edit, and she still had to make sure the other panel members delivered!

"O'Connor Design." . . . "Hey! I was going to call you. You know I'm leaving Friday, right?" . . . "Actually, I can't talk now. I'm crazy-busy! " . . . "Hmmm. Sure, tonight's fine." . . . "What's up? Are you okay? " . . . "Good. Should I bring anything?". . . "Okay, see you then. Ciao!"

Lorraine put the phone down and stared at it.

Max was playing downtown and wouldn't be home until four in the morning. So she'd planned to finish at least one of the jobs hanging over her head. And the second one tomorrow. She could edit her paper Tuesday - Wednesday, and finish it on the plane. Early Thursday night she'd touch base with the other panel members. Then spend the evening with Max after he got home from a gig. Since she was leaving Friday morning, he would be coming home early.

Lorraine tapped one bright red manicured nail on her desk. Julie sounded like something was bothering her. Her best friend had been hit hard by her grandmother's death. Maybe that was it.

So while Lorraine didn't have time, she would make time. She couldn't leave not knowing her best friend was okay.

But why did Julie have to pick this week?!

THIRTEEN

VIRGIN AMAZON

"I'm so sorry about Gran."

Julie nodded. "I know. She looked so good the night before, I thought she might recover."

"Are you all right?"

"No, I'm not."

"You will be."

"Thanks for coming over. I didn't want to be alone tonight."

Julie and Lorraine had just finished dinner. They were still sitting at the table, Lorraine sipping the last of her wine, Julie silently sculpting little mountains from some barley and rice on her plate.

"The lamb was great!"

Julie smiled. "The recipe I stole from Michener's *Caravan*."

Lorraine glanced comfortably around Julie's studio apartment, until she came to the family photos. One of her grandmother, three of her dad.

The son of a bitch.

Disappearing on a six year old. And what, more than twelve years later? She still worships her father. When was Julie going to get it? And move on?

One photo showed him standing in the garden at Norwood, looking down at a wild bird perched on his hand. Lorraine knew the story. How he'd cared for a young bird that had fallen from its nest until it could fly. How nice. But what about his own daughter?

In the picture, his eyes dark and mysterious, handsome as a movie star. A man in his rolled up white shirt sleeves taming a wild thing. A gentle, quiet stillness about him. No wonder his daughter was so entranced by him.

But he was still a son of a bitch.

The second picture was taken during the war. In uniform, grinning, he looked care-free and irresistible. In the third photo he sat in a row boat with young Julie. Both of them holding fishing poles and grinning.

"Handsome man," Lorraine commented thoughtfully, thinking he seemed so nice.

"Beautiful mom, handsome dad," Julie answered.

"Still writing those letters?" Lorraine asked.

"To my father?"

"No, the Pope." Lorraine rolled her eyes.

"Now and then."

"You write to someone you haven't seen in more than twelve years. Someone who abandoned you, your mother, and his own mother. You don't know where to mail them. You don't even know if he's still alive."

Lorraine made a face. "It's like writing to a ghost."

"He's not someone. He's my father! And no, I don't know

where to send them. And I don't know if he's dead or alive, but I have seen him."

Lorraine stared at her friend. "What?"

"I keep thinking I see him. On the street, in a crowd. He might be dead by now."

"You know, whether he's alive or dead, your seeing him all the time could mean he really wants to contact you."

"I can't believe you said that." As long as she'd known her, Lorraine didn't have a mystical bone in her body.

Lorraine shook her head. "I wouldn't call it *supernatural*. Just something we don't understand. Like when you think of someone and then they call you. We just don't know how that works yet. "

"So you believe in telepathy?"

"Maybe. But I don't think it's supernatural."

"But I still think you writing those letters is sick." Then waving her hands to erase what she'd just said. "Unhealthy. Not good for you."

Julie stood up and started clearing the table. Holding one dinner plate in each hand, she looked at her friend dead on. "It comforts me."

Lorraine got up too, to help her clear. "I know. But that doesn't mean it's good for you," she said, following Julie into the kitchen.

It was small and narrow but Lorraine knew where everything went and felt completely at home.

She handed the glasses and silverware to Julie who started rinsing them. Tenement apartments did not come with dishwashers, nor was there room for one. As Julie washed the dishes, Lorraine slid behind her and put the salt and pepper shakers on a spice shelf and the butter in the fridge.

"Lorraine, I don't care if it's healthy or not. I wish I'd never told you I wrote to him."

"Right. Hide what you do from your best friend. Great idea!"

"Stop worrying about me. I'm fine."

"I'm not worried. I just wish you'd move on."

Julie took a deep breath. "I'm okay. I know seeing him is just wishful thinking. What's harder are the dreams."

"What dreams?"

"Nightmares."

I'm a monstrous girl covered with gaping wounds sewn together badly

Julie's hands gripped the edge of the sink. She did not plan to tell Lor about that one. Not now. Maybe never.

"I dream about my father. You know he drove a bus."

"Sure."

"I dream I'm waiting for a bus and he drives right by me. Or he's driving the bus I'm riding, but he goes past my stop. I ring the bell over and over but he doesn't hear me." Julie bit her lip and felt the old heart ache. "Or I give him a transfer and he says it's no good. So, he makes me get off the bus and I'm completely lost. I don't know where I am."

Julie laughed sadly, "Sometimes, he won't let me on the bus! Or, he keeps handing me a transfer like I should just go away." She shook her head and swiped at her eyes. "The worst thing? He never knows me."

Lorraine handed her a paper towel.

Julie dried her eyes and hands. "Pathetic."

"No," Lorraine said, as she put her arms around her friend and gave her a brief hug. "Pretty damn sad, I'd say.

"Come on, not to change the subject, and I probably shouldn't ask, but I was wondering . . . "

Julie blew her nose into the paper towel and tossed it into the trash. "What?"

"Are you still making those little dead ladies?"

Julie stared at her until she saw Lorraine's mischievous grin. Julie smiled back, then reached down, scooped up some soap suds, and smirking flung them at her friend who knew better and ducked in time.

"Leave the mummies alone, will you? Look, I may not strangle you, but you are definitely in danger of no dessert. What do you want, chocolate ice cream or raspberry sorbet?"

"Both!"

"Why do I bother to ask?"

Julie started a kettle for tea, while Lorraine got the two pints out of the freezer. "Have you ever considered defrosting your fridge?"

"Not until it becomes absolutely necessary."

"Looks pretty serious to me."

"Once I went a whole year. That's my record."

"You can't fit any food in there! It's all ice!"

"You exaggerate. Come on. Let's have dessert."

Sitting at the table, Lorraine swirled her chocolate ice cream and raspberry sorbet together as Julie took small spoonfuls first from one and then the other.

"Well, are you?"

Julie sighed. "I started working on another one the other day but I don't know when I'll get back to it."

"Why, what's keeping you from the little dead guys?"

"Maybe Gran's death."

"Sorry."

"And don't call them that. They're female, for one thing. And you sound like Ed."

Pointing her spoon at Julie and jabbing the air, Lorraine said, "Don't even mention me in the same sentence with that creep! I will never say a mean thing about your Weird Ladies again. I promise.

"Hey! Maybe he's history?"

"Not yet. I can't handle dealing with him right now."

Lorraine shrugged. "You don't ever have to see him again if you don't want to."

"We're having dinner tomorrow night."

"Why? I don't get it! Why see him at all if you don't want to? I only met him once, and he gave me the creeps. I'm serious. Okay, he's a scientist. Smart. Dresses well. Takes you nice places. The externals are fine. But there's something very wrong with that fellow."

Julie nodded slowly.

"What exactly does he do?"

"He . . . I don't know. Experiments. Every time I ask him about his work, he changes the subject."

"That's reassuring." Lorraine swirled her spoon in the last of her dessert. "He scares me actually."

"Yeah, and you don't scare easy!" Julie teased.

Lorraine, still serious, said quietly, "No, I don't."

"I'm going to end it."

"Where's your phone?"

"I want to tell him face to face."

"You don't have to be nice to Mr. Scary Weird Guy."

But Julie felt she did. *And why was that?*

"So, what does he think of the mummies?"

Julie frowned. "He doesn't like them. But you don't either."

"Face it, they're not what most people want to hang over the couch to brighten up a room."

"Very funny."

"You think I'm kidding?"

"What about these paintings," Lorraine said, gesturing toward two Julie had hung in her apartment. "Does he like them? I love them! They're so colorful, so cheerful!"

"Ed's never been here."

"You have others from this series at the loft. He's been there, right?"

"Just once."

"Well, what did he say? Their gorgeous!"

Five feet square, and yes, one hung over her couch, the other over her bed. Paintings from her earlier playful *Maps & Games* series. Each a painted collage of favorite images of hers: big black and white dominoes, bright yellow puzzle pieces, blue and white star maps, a large base clef, a white horse that might be a weather vane or from a carousel. An old fashioned locomotive, a cross word puzzle, a labyrinth of crochet, and clouds, fluffy painterly clouds.

Each had taken a month of work. Sometimes fourteen hour days. None of the dealers had offered her a show, yet. Maybe someday. For now, she enjoyed them. And Lor did too.

Since then, her paintings had gotten progressively darker. And smaller. Although she felt her *New York by Moonlight* series apart from the muted colors, all in greys, and browns and black and white had a radiance given the ever present full moon. And now the mummies, her little Death Dolls. And worse, a painting of a young dead girl screaming. And no, she was not going to tell Lor about the night she painted that one. Or about the painting. She'd never done anything like it before.

A young dead girl screaming

"Earth to Julie." Lorraine lit a cigarette.

"Sorry. I was drifting."

"What's bothering you?"

"Nothing."

"Right," deciding not to press.

"So what did Ed say when he saw one of these paintings?"

Julie got up and opened a window, then returned to the table wishing Lorraine would stop smoking. "He didn't say anything but he took pictures of them."

"Where do you get these guys? Let me ask you something. Is he wild about you? That's what I really want to know."

"We only went out twice. But, you know what is odd about him?"

"He has two?" Lorraine grinned impishly.

Julie rolled her eyes and laughed. "I wouldn't know."

"Aw, he only has one?"

Julie gave her a look.

"I'm listening," Lorraine answered, suddenly serious.

"He wants a key to my loft."

"What? I thought you said he hates the loft."

"He does. He called it filthy, rat infested, and disgusting."

"It's not dirty. And you don't have rats there, do you?"

Julie shook her head.

"It's not disgusting. Just an unrenovated loft."

"I know. He asks me how can I work there, and then he asks for a key."

"You did not give him one, right?"

Julie shook her head. "I told him I'm there to work. When he calls and I don't pick up, he's always furious."

"How do you know?"

"Because of his messages, and he also always tells me so the first chance he gets."

The two women looked at each other silently for a few beats. Lorraine said, "That's what I mean."

"He wants a key to my loft, but won't show me his lab," Julie added.

"Why not?"

"He's got a different reason every time I ask."

"You'd think he'd be proud to have his own lab in a prestigious place like the Institute. You'd think he couldn't wait to take you there and show off a little."

That's just what Julie thought. Lorraine was her best friend, but when Julie began to notice Ed's strangeness, instead of telling Lor, she found she began to cut corners on the truth. Why did she do that?

It was like she didn't want to face the obvious. She hadn't been ready, until tonight, to let her friend's objectivity cut through her own denial.

"I wonder what he's hiding," Lorraine said, sounding even more concerned.

Julie laughed. "He's not Dracula."

"Right. He's the one with the cape and the unusual over-bite. This one sounds more like Victor Frankenstein. What?"

"Nothing."

"Well, I'd begin to worry when he did invite me to see that lab."

"I'm not going to see him anymore."

"You're seeing him tomorrow night!"

"Just one more time."

"Be careful."

"I will." But why did she choose so badly?

Lorraine grinned. "Face it, Ed's not exactly husband material."

"You know I don't want to get married."

"You just have to meet the right guy. Remember how I was?"

"You didn't strike me as wife material."

"Love, Julie. That's what does it."

"So they say."

"You'll meet him. And it would help, if you didn't wear black, head to foot, morning, noon, and night! No wonder you attract vampires."

"Just because you found someone wonderful, doesn't mean I will," Julie snapped. She hated false hope, and it seemed to her that Lorraine, so happily married, could not imagine anything but a happy ending for her.

"You will. Virgin Amazons are always right!"

"Lorraine, you are not a virgin."

"Not anymore, but I was! I was a *Love Virgin*. Like you."

Julie sighed, but smiled.

"To be continued," Lorraine said, as she pushed her chair away from the table and walked over to Julie's bed to get her coat. I've got to go. I've still got so much to do!"

Lorraine slipped her coat on, shouldered her bag, and pulled on her gloves. "Again, I'm so sorry about Gran. But you do know she would want you to be happy."

"I know."

"And I'm relieved to know that creep will finally be out of your life soon. But one more thing. You won't want to hear it, but unfortunately I feel I'm right, so please listen? Because I'm really worried about you."

"What?" Steeling herself already.

"If you don't find a way to get past your dad's disappearing on you, you are never going to have a life, or find love." Lorraine expected Julie might get angry, but she didn't.

Instead, she said quietly, "I know. But the only way I think I can get past it is if I understand what happened, and I don't see how I'm going to find that out. Unless he comes back someday. And after all this time, I know, I really know, how unlikely that is. I just can't give up hope."

Lorraine nodded. "You don't have to. I just want you to be happy."

"I know."

Seeing that Julie had actually heard her and not brushed her off, Lor decided to change the subject.

"Well, it's going to be a crazy week," but we'll talk before I go."

At the door, Lorraine pointed to a small New York by Moonlight painting hung in Julie's narrow foyer. "I love these, too." They kissed on the cheek and gave each other a warm hug. "You know, with your father, it was a good thing you had your mother, at least for a while. But you never talk about her."

Julie winced and clutched her stomach.

"Are you all right?"

"I think. . . I have to. . . ." Julie ran for the bathroom.

Lorraine heard her throw up.

When she came out, Lorraine said, "I feel fine so it couldn't be the lamb. Maybe you've got a touch of flu?"

"I don't think so. I feel better now."

"Look, chin up. We'll get together as soon as I get back but I might stay a few more days after the conference to see some of Italy. I'll call you before I go." At the door, Lorraine hugged Julie again.

"Ciao!"she waved, with a big smile just as she stepped into the elevator.

Julie did her best to smile and wave back. When the elevator door closed, she closed her door, locked both locks and dropped the chain into position, thinking how odd it was her getting sick like that, just then.

FOURTEEN

THE ROSEWOOD BOX

By the time Julie had gotten home from the loft, Ed had left three messages begging her to forgive him. She did not return those calls. And was glad Lor came over.

Ed frightened her now. One minute he bullied. The next, he begged. If that didn't work he flattered. Doctor Jekyll and Mr. Hyde. Ed was intelligent, yes, and charming, at first.

By the second date he seemed vaguely dissatisfied and had odd mood swings. She thought he might be frustrated by something at the lab. She kept an open mind. Tried to be understanding.

In other words, she bared her throat.

Big mistake.

And after all the movies she'd watched, she thought she would have recognized a certain type of vampire.

He had been changing before her eyes, or maybe just taking off his disguise, bit by bit. A horrific striptease she had watched in disbelief. His initial attentive demeanor had become a constant critical scowl. Dr. Edward Henry was no longer pleased and it was her fault, as he made clear.

At first, she made an effort to bring back the guy who had been so bright and interesting.

I'll be good daddy! Daddy come back!

It didn't work.

His initial interest quickly became constant criticism of her work, demands for a key to her loft, and that she be in constant contact with him.

It all happened so fast it was bizarre. But worst of all, when Mr. Hyde leered from center stage, something dark deep within her slipped into place. She was home.

Home sweet terrifying home.

She would tell him not to call her ever again, but she couldn't deal with that tonight. She would see him one more time, tomorrow night, and get it over with.

They were going out to dinner. Nothing too terrible could happen in a restaurant. The way things were going they would probably argue and that would give her the perfect reason to leave, and never see him again.

But what could she do now to take her mind off him tonight? She wasn't sleepy yet.

She glanced around her apartment for inspiration, and seeing the lovely carved rosewood box sitting atop her bureau she remembered the manuscript her grandmother had given her. The box containing the curling vellum manuscript and a large porcelain cup hand-painted by Gran long ago with leafy blueberry branches, were all Julie had brought back from Norwood to her apartment. She wanted them home with her, not knowing when she would get up to the house again; maybe not until spring.

As soon as she'd returned, she put the cup on top of her bureau surrounded by her hair brush, photographs of Gran and her father, and one of Monet in his garden. She had placed the beautiful antique box on top of her bureau, too, and in her grief, forgotten it.

For the first time since Gran's funeral, Julie felt interested in something. So like Gran to want to surprise her. But what a strange gift! Was the manuscript really authentic? Would she be holding in her hands the original pages of Mary Shelley's *Frankenstein* written in her own hand?

Not likely. Although Gran said it had been in the family since the 1850's and Julie had no reason to doubt her. Even if the manuscript was a forgery, that would be interesting too. But who would do such a thing? And why?

She remembered reading somewhere that the novel, *Frankenstein*, had been rejected by both Percy Shelley's and Byron's publishers, but once published by a small firm it was a great success, so maybe someone somehow had forged a copy of the manuscript right away, trying to cash in. Or, in the era before copier machines, much less computers, Mary may have simply made a copy for herself.

Julie walked over to her bureau. Took the antique key on its chain out of the cup. Picked up the box and carried it to her coffee table where she sat down on her couch, held it in her lap, and unlocked it.

Once again she admired the exquisite carving of the roses, leaves and the vines with faint traces of what must be almost two hundred year old paint and glittering gold leaf.

Then she went into the kitchen to pour herself a glass of apple juice.

Since it was already after ten, she decided to make herself comfortable first. Even dress for the occasion. It was, after all, her grandmother's parting gift. And what if it really was the original manuscript of Mary Shelley's *Frankenstein!*

After a quick shower, she changed into a pale blue flannel nightgown. Then, as a treat, she opened her closet, unzipped a plastic dust cover, and took out a robe, one a kind older saleswoman at Macy's had urged her to buy instead of the plain grey flannel she'd been about to try on. So she returned home with a robe the romantic in her found utterly beautiful. And never regretted changing her mind.

She slipped into the floor length full sleeved blue velvet robe, with quilted satin cuffs and a matching yoke. The high, round collar tied with generous lengths of velvet cords, so she made an extravagant bow. And there were slippers to match.

Never worn. Neither the robe nor the slippers. Saved for some undefined special occasion that never happened. But tonight, they seemed perfect for reading what claimed to be a nineteenth century manuscript.

She sat on the couch, unlocked the box, and slowly lifted the heavy lid for the first time.

Just for tonight, she would pretend the pages inside were the original manuscript of Mary Shelley's *Frankenstein* written in her own hand.

Comfortable on the couch, her long hair fastened with a clip into a loose knot, and in her blue velvet robe looking very like a nineteenth century romantic, Julie carefully picked up the manuscript and gazed down at the pages.

It certainly looked authentic. And if it were? Here was a past she could hold in her hands. The ink might once have been a deeper blue and the sheets of paper a creamy white, but now the ink had faded and the paper yellowed with age.

Could this really be the original manuscript of Frankenstein? Written in Mary Shelley's own hand?

Julie felt her heart leap with excitement, then laughed at herself. Couldn't be.

Well, she would just sit back and enjoy it.

Frankenstein, Or The Modern Prometheus, by Mary Shelley written across the first page.

Julie smiled and found herself taking a deep breath.

Just for tonight, she would believe.

FIFTEEN

THE MANUSCRIPT

Julie enjoyed reading the first few pages of Mary Shelley's *Frankenstein,* a book she hadn't read since high school, but Gran was right. Everyone knows the story. And if this manuscript was authentic she shouldn't even be touching it.

She would have experts decide, and if it was authentic, she would donate it to a collection where it would be properly taken care of and made available to scholars. For now, she placed the manuscript back inside the beautiful box, and sipped her apple juice.

But her gaze kept returning to the rosewood box sitting right in front of her on the coffee table.

She pulled the box onto her lap. There was something wrong with the proportions of the box given the space inside.

The few traces of shining gold leaf that clung to the carved vines and roses winked at her as she lifted the box up to eye level to examine the thick base. She turned it upside down, looking closely. Righting it, she pulled the first drawer out and laid it on the couch. She slipped her hand inside to make sure nothing had got caught at the back of the drawer.

Nothing.

Except the baseboard shifted a little.

She pressed down and tried to draw it forward. It resisted. But little by little, she eased it forward, and as it moved, her fingertips touched paper.

A bundle of paper.

Wow!

She took care withdrawing it.

On the first page, boldly penned in the same handwriting as the other manuscript:

From Darkness
My True Account
by
Mary Shelley

What is this?

The handwriting was hard to read. Not neatly written like the *Frankenstein* manuscript. Words were crossed out or inserted. A phrase circled with an arrow pointed where it should move. Barely any space between lines. The script leaned far forward as if she couldn't write fast enough. The letters in each word close upon its neighbor. The letter t crossed the entire length of the word. Unashamed splotches of ink. The story rushing out of her.

It began with a quote. "Till this ghastly tale is told, this heart within me burns." *The Ancient Mariner*, by Samuel Taylor Coleridge.

How exciting! A true account? Some sort of hidden diary?

But as Julie began to read, she frowned.

SIXTEEN

GENEVA, SWITZERLAND (1816)

In the middle of May, during an unseasonably late and heavy snowstorm in the Jura Mountains, four young travelers arrived at the Hôtel d'Angleterre, on the shore of Lake Geneva.

The party had been forced to hire four extra horses and ten men to pull their carriage through the deep snow in the mountains; the roads invisible, the forest impenetrable.

They arrived at the hotel at twilight. One of them confiding to her journal that night wrote, "Never was scene more awfully desolate."

These daring English travelers were a nineteen year old mother, Mary Godwin, accompanied by the twenty-four year old poet Percy Shelley, their four-month-old son, William, and Mary's step-sister, Claire Clairmont, also nineteen. Mary had not yet written her novel *Frankenstein*. However, she would begin the book this spring and complete it the following year. When she and Percy married she would become known as Mary Shelley.

For ten days, they rested from their harsh and exhausting journey through the Jura mountains.

Claire, however, was impatient and filled with excitement, awaiting the arrival of her one time lover, the notorious poet, Lord Byron.

While winter raged in the higher altitudes, the weather below in this Alpine basin was a brisk spring promising summer. Wild flowers bravely thrusting and blooming through the last thin crust of snow.

On the far shore of Lake Geneva, across the lake from the Hôtel d'Angleterre, a chalet called Maison Chapuis comfortably sheltered by a grove of pine trees, and amicably surrounded by an ancient rambling vineyard, nestled near the water with its own harbor and a small sail boat.

Behind the chalet, and a short walk up the hill, with a superb view of the magnificent Alps encircling the lake, stood a much grander establishment, the Villa Diodati.

About the chalet and the villa, the wind soughed through a fragrant stand of tall dark pine trees. The ground soft with the pine needles of many past autumns.

After the three travelers deliberated regarding the length of their projected stay, Shelley rented Maison Chapuis and the sail boat. All that was required was a day or two for the owners to freshen the fully furnished rooms. Mary hired a Swiss maid, Elise, to help her with William, and to clean and cook for the four of them.

At four o'clock on their first day at the chalet, the sun was warm, the sky clear. A light and tantalizing wind skittered across the lake.

Delighted, Shelley went for a sail.

Mary and Claire remained at the cottage with baby William and Elise, arranging things to suit them.

SEVENTEEN

CHILL

"Mary, when will he arrive?"

Claire paced the sitting-room, her long russet gown rustling at every turn, and each time she passed the mirror, she glanced into it, each time with a different expression.

Just now, she looked most earnest and inquiring.

Mary knew better than to reply.

"We have been here ten long days," Claire declared to the glass. "What a perfectly infuriating man!" A smile played across her pretty mouth. But when she passed the mirror again, her lips were pouting, her brow furrowed. Claire wanted to be an actress, but no one took her seriously. Did they know she was acting all the time? Even now?

No, it wouldn't occur to them. Neither Mary nor Percy had any time for play. Always with their noses in a book! She knew they pitied her, thought her brain not as good as theirs. But with all their learning, they couldn't've guessed, how thoroughly boring she found them.

"Mary, when will he arrive? How will he find me, I wonder. Mary, answer me! Pray, say something!"

Here, the face in the mirror appeared quite innocent of any knowledge of how it might be perceived. Only the strained voice, faltering as it escaped the mirror's net, proclaimed itself vexed. Claire might have been stamping her foot.

"Surely, Claire, you do not believe that I've the power to foretell the appearance of Lord Byron?" Mary continued to unpack her books, arranging them in an oak bookcase she had moved next to a small French writing desk she planned to work at during their stay. On the desk, she placed her own well-read editions of Petrarch, Milton, and Goethe to the right, and on the left hand side of the desk, several volumes of the popular fiction of the day, that Shelley abhorred, but she much enjoyed.

"Claire, only think, just a few years ago, you and I were children together, hiding behind the sofa, discovered, and almost sent to bed. Do you remember?"

Claire remembered, quite pleased by the memory. "But I begged and pleaded so prettily, because I knew you wanted to hear that dreary poem, and I wanted to see if the gentlemen would plead in our favor and force my mother to allow us to have our way! And they did! They did!"

Claire clapped her hands, jubilant in memory's reflection, while Mary, who had seated herself in a rocking chair, seemed to look back that far distance more pensively, looking back through the years to that candlelit night, as she began to recite from the poem aloud.

> "It is an ancient Mariner,
> And he stoppeth one of three.
> By thy long grey beard and glittering eye,
> Now wherefore stopp'st me?"

Rocking slowly in the chair she continued.

'Like one who on a lonely road,

Does walk in fear and dread,

And having once turned round walks on,

turns no more his head.

Because he knows a frightful fiend

doth close behind him tread.'"

"Mary! How can you remember all that? And why would you want to?"

"Well, I believe, it belongs to me."

Claire's eyes grew large and incredulous, then, lowering her head bullishly, she fisted both hands on her hips, and with blazing eyes confronted her step-sister.

"Don't make fun of me, Mary! You never wrote that! We were only nine years old. It was that old man's poem, I am sure of it!"

By now, Claire was pacing back and forth again, pounding her small fist into the palm of her hand, her complexion flushed with vexation. "What was his name?"

"Mr. Coleridge. Those are two verses from his poem, "The Rime of the Ancient Mariner," Mary answered quietly, calm as ever. This was her nature, but it was a manner that infuriated volatile Claire. Mary's eyes were thoughtful as they gazed across the chasm that had always separated her from her step-sister, and from most other people as well, until Shelley.

"Claire, I never said I wrote that poem."

"You said it was yours. What did you expect me to think?"

"I am truly sorry, Claire. I did not mean to upset you and I never meant to laugh at you. Please believe me."

Claire seated herself on the window seat and began to smooth the folds of her dress. When she had finished making her arrangements, her face was calm. "I believe you, Mary," she replied, looking out over the lake as she spoke, presenting her best profile.

Of course, she believed no such thing. What did Mary take her for? "It's just that you and Shelley are ever so clever, and no matter how much I read, I shall never catch up with the two of you. Of course, most of what the two of you read, I find completely boring. But you always had a taste for that sort of thing, even as a child, like that old man's beastly poem! But Mary, in God's name tell me, why did you call it yours?"

Mary rose from the rocking chair and reached into her valise to unpack her writing paper, quill pen, and ink, arranging them on her desk as she replied. "Well, Claire, you may have a good laugh at me if you like, because I really do not know.

"I only know that "The Rime of The Ancient Mariner" in some way belongs to me, and I to it.

"Those verses haunt me so, I feel certain, that this poem of a deathly ship is the key to a door I would rather die than unlock."

"Mary, if you keep going on like that you will frighten me!"

"Well," Mary said with a laugh, "I suppose I have succeeded in frightening myself. Is it not chill now Claire, all of a sudden?"

"Yes, chill and damp."

"Here, Claire, take your shawl and I shall put on mine as well."

She could take care of the cold, and she would. "I will have Elise make a fire for us."

Comfortable in taking reasonable action, Mary left the sitting room for the nursery.

Claire drew her shawl snugly about herself and walked slowly over to the window that faced west. She gazed out across the lake to the hotel, at the last brilliant rays of the setting sun, feeling lost and uncertain.

EIGHTEEN

WALKING ON WATER

Mary, Shelley, and Claire dined that night in the sitting room, having a late dinner of soup, bread, cheese, and fruit. Elise had served them, and now sat by the hearth feeding baby William.

"Only think," Claire said, "he may arrive at any moment! How do I look? I think I am pale."

Shelley received a note that day from Lord Byron, posted from the Rhine Valley. He wrote them he hoped to arrive by the twenty-first of May and had rented the nearby Villa Diodati for his stay. This evening was the twenty-third.

But Mary and Percy assumed that Byron and his doctor, Polidori, were delayed by the same heavy snow they had encountered in the mountains.

Shelley said, "It is quite likely we shall see them both sometime tomorrow."

Claire frowned. Tore at her bread, but ate nothing. "And then, he made no mention of me," she continued, "of our particular relation. But I am certain Lord Byron, being such a great gentleman and poet, has considered the delicacy of my feelings, and means to speak to me privately."

Claire looked up at Mary and Shelley, smiling shyly, while they exchanged glances with each other without expression.

They both knew, Claire having confided in them, that several months ago, she had sent yet another note to the famous poet, the Sixth Lord Byron of Newstead. On that occasion she risked more than before:

'If a woman, whose reputation has yet remained unstained, without either guardian or husband to control her should throw herself upon your Mercy with a beating heart and confess the Love she has bourne you, if she should secure to you secrecy and safety, and return your Kindness with fond Affection and unbounded Devotion, could you betray her, or would you be silent as the grave?'

Byron had recently decided upon a permanent separation from his wife and child. At the same time, there were rumors rampant of an incestuous relation between him and his half-sister, Augusta. By all accounts true, the rumor managed to appall even the most sophisticated in society. As a result, he had been insulted in the street on his way to the House of Lords, cold-shouldered at parties, and stoned in the press. In a rage, he decided to flee to the Continent, a furious self-imposed exile.

However, just one week before his planned departure, Byron received Claire's note. Although she had been writing to him for over a year, this was the first time she signed her name. On two occasions, she had come to his door and been turned away by the servants. She wrote again, and again. And finally,

"... I do not expect you to Love me. I am not worthy of your Love ... Have you any objection to the following plan ... ?"

He was leaving in a week with no thought of return. Surrounded by derision, poisoned by his own fury, no, Lord Byron had no objection whatsoever.

At the age of twenty-eight, Byron had achieved a vivid reputation as a dazzling poet. Tall, slim, and handsome, with a fair complexion, coppery red hair, and blue-grey eyes, he had an ardent, fierce, and extravagant nature, a brilliant mind, and a violent temper. Even with the club foot he had been born with, women found him irresistible. But in truth, he was a man's man and much preferred the hunt or a night of debated argument in the company of men, to society and its breed of masked players.

However, society made it clear it would not tolerate incest between Byron and his half-sister.

Even the suspicion of its truth had rendered him outcast.

Claire was half right. Lord Byron had garnered quite a reputation, but it was not for that of a gentleman.

Regardless of their nights together, she was to him, if he thought of her at all, only a delightful memory, and Claire would be painfully mistaken if she hoped for something more. Pretty, vivacious, and considering herself emancipated, even so, Claire Clairmont was no match for the most brilliant, passionate, and cynical man of her time.

Mary felt pity and compassion for the girl who seemed to have no idea how ill-suited she and Byron were. Shelley sighed, feeling powerless to prevent Claire's feelings from being hurt.

Neither Mary, nor Shelley, knew why Claire must hope. For, since her night with Byron, Claire was pregnant.

After dinner, Mary took William from Elise and sat on the floor with him near the fire, while Elise cleared the table.

Shelley chose a comfortable chair and pulled it closer to Mary and William. Claire paced the length of the room, pulling her shawl close about her. Now and then, she glanced out the windows overlooking the moonlit lake.

At night, the cold from the mountains descended into the valley. When darkness settled in outside the Maison Chapuis, a relentless wind battered the cottage's windows.

Over by the fire, Mary fashioned a crown for William from a sheet of writing paper and placed it on his head. The baby shrieked with delight.

"Ah, Your Highness!" Shelly's blue eyes danced. "Good evening, Your Highness!" Shelley smiled and bowed from his chair to the baby.

William looked happily from Percy to Mary, then quickly pulled the crown from his head, and fisted it toward his mouth.

"No, William!" Mary laughed, as she pulled the baby up off the floor and unto her lap. Tickling him to divert him, he dropped the paper crown.

"There is always someone at the hotel, isn't there?" Claire wondered aloud, staring hard out the windows across the lake. "What if he should arrive now? Would he stay at the hotel, Mary, or take the boat and come to us straight away?"

"Claire, I should think they would try to discourage any crossing at this hour. It would surely be dangerous."

Shelley laughed. "And I am certain the two of them will want nothing more than a pint or two and a warm bed when they arrive.

"We should all retire and rest, in light of what promises to be an intriguing visit for all of us."

"I shall copy his poems for him."

Mary and Shelley exchanged another glance.

"Claire, come sit with us by the fire," invited Shelley.

Mary walked over to the window, carrying William. He was beginning to rub his eyes, nuzzling into her neck.

"And what do you think Shelley, wouldn't it be glorious!" Claire danced before Shelley.

"What would be glorious, Claire?"

"Why, Byron might write a play for me!" Claire was hugging herself, twirling before the fire.

Holding William in her arms, Mary gazed out the windows that overlooked Lake Geneva. The moonlight made the lake look like an enormous bowl of milk fit for a giant. Smiling, at her whimsy, she kissed William's wisp of hair and was turning away from the windows to check the fire when she saw something.

What was that on the lake? A man walking on the glittering waters? She hugged William close. Asleep, he sighed deeply.

"Well, if he won't, you'll write a play for me, won't you, Shelley?" Claire had stopped twirling. She sat at Shelley's feet, her small white hand resting on his slippered foot.

Unconsciously, Mary might have noticed that Claire, in lieu of her absent love, was once again flirting with Shelley, but Mary was so curious regarding what she thought she had just seen, she took little notice of them.

The night had painted the surrounding trees and vineyard the deepest ebony. The moonlight laced them with silver, as swiftly moving clouds created a kaleidoscope of shadows that gamboled across the lake.

She thought she saw a man walking on the water, his arms outstretched. Perhaps the vision had been a trick of moonlight and cloud shadows.

But Mary Godwin was a careful observer. She had seen something like an apparition advancing across the lake. But that could not be. So, she must look again, and more closely.

After a moment, she decided it must have been a suggestive shadow.

Mary glanced over her shoulder at Shelley and Claire.

Claire had put the baby's crown on Shelley's head and was clapping and laughing. Shelley was laughing, too.

Instinctively, Mary started to walk back toward them, when once more she thought she saw something. There, through the window, his arms describing broad gestures, the man no longer walked on water but stood on the pier. A smaller man, beside him, appeared to be paying the boatman.

"Shelley! Claire! Lord Byron has surprised us."

Claire shrieked and ran up the stairs to her room, calling back to them, "Tell him I am sleeping!" Mary gave the stirring baby to Elise. She and Shelley threw their cloaks over their shoulders and went down to the beach to greet their guests.

Lord Byron shouted, "As we crossed, I waved to you!"

"You appeared to be walking on the water, Lord Byron." Shelley looked at Mary with interest.

"How amusing," remarked Dr. Polidori.

"In the moonlight," Byron said dreamily, "your cottage looked a ghostly gleaming white, as if it were made of sugar in some marvelous, murderous fairy tale. Is it haunted?" He limped briskly, using his cane for broad expansive gestures.

"We have not had an apparition as yet," quipped Shelley, "but what fun if we should. We might interrogate it in a scientific manner." Shelley was only half joking as he excitedly walked ahead of everyone, walking backward, eager to enter into Mary and Byron's conversation.

"Well, we should take precautions against arousing any demons. What do you say, physician?" Lord Byron's cape snapped in the strong winds. His red-gold hair a tangled mass of curls. Mary stepped away from him. She hoped he didn't notice.

"There is no scientific evidence for demons, Lord Byron."

"My God, some of you scientific men are such bores!" Byron limped gamely, head held high, his broad shoulders magnificent in his velvet cloak. "I haven't frightened you, my dear?"

Mary met his gaze but did not answer. He turned away at once.

"And you, Shelley, what is your opinion of demons? Do they exist?" The older poet's powerful voice and body, his lively facial expressions, all pulsed with life.

The infamous Lord Byron fairly glowed like a lantern in the dark, Mary thought, his eyes flickering as if bolts of lightning flashed within him.

"I agree with Polidori," Shelley answered. "Sometimes the truth is boring. But I am broad-minded. Perhaps ghosts can be explained scientifically. You see, I am an atheist. For me, there is no God. No Devil either. Only human beings and their dark ways that science has only begun to cast some light upon."

"And you, Mary Godwin," the poet turned and gazed again in her direction. The eagle circling.

"What is your opinion, for I am sure you have one."

Mary walked along attending to the stones beneath her feet," as she considered her answer. "Lord Byron, I have never found truth to be boring, and while I welcome the light of reason, I would fear an explanation of evil, if we thought we had done with it so easily."

"Aha! So, you believe in demons?"

"Do you?"

"My estate is haunted, you know. Has been for centuries. A perfectly harmless monk, I have become quite used to him."

The party made their way from the pier to the cottage.

While Elise took their cloaks, Mary surveyed the pantry for a quick tea.

Suddenly, quite tired, she had no desire to begin a new acquaintance at this late hour.

She instructed Elise as to serving, and bid the gentlemen goodnight.

As she ascended the stairs to hers and Percy's bedroom, she heard his rather high pitched exuberant voice. "Perhaps, there is a scientific equivalent for good and evil?"

The grave, musical voice of Lord Byron responded, but Mary could no longer hear what he said.

Poor Claire, Mary reflected. The handsome and vigorous Lord Byron made no mention of her at all.

NINETEEN

EVENING

"Scurrying little animals,
preening and biting.
Eating berries, drinking blood.
There's such a rustling
in the forest these days."
Book of Forgetfulness
Anonymous

It was a day when every living thing yearned for rain.

The mountains thundering as brilliant lightening struck the snowy Alpine peaks again and again.

By seven, that evening, Mary heard the wind swoop down from the mountains, seeing it billow the drapery before her bedroom window. The tall dark stand of pines, surrounding Maison Chapuis, tossing in the wind like distressed dreamers.

Mary had felt restless all day.

She tried reading Petrarch, but history suddenly seemed so far away and unreasonable, even incomprehensible. She opened a volume of Shakespeare, but the words, instead of absorbing or amusing her, sprawled across the page, like peevish actors refusing to perform.

Even baby William had been restless, mysteriously inconsolable, worrying Mary as she thought of Maie, her baby girl who had not survived.

Claire wandered about like a sleepwalker, stunned by Byron's neglect; while Shelley was as excited as a schoolboy with his new, stimulating friend. Even now, Byron and he, having abandoned the staid Polidori, were sailing the choppy waters of Lake Geneva.

Mary chose her best gown to wear this evening. Byron having rented the grand and venerable Villa Diodati, invited her and Shelley to dine with him tonight, including Claire and Polidori.

Mary knew why she was restless.

Although she made a strong effort to restrain her thoughts, irresistible daydreams were riddling her mind and heart with the strength of determined vines that will force their way through stone.

And she had found, to her disquiet, sensuous blooms bursting from that vine of reverie initiated by the handsome poet's dramatic arrival.

Mary opened the armoire where her few gowns hung, to admire the one she would wear that evening. A twilight blue silk and matching silk slippers.

She had told Elise they would all be at the Villa for dinner and might be quite late. Elise need not wait up for them. William had finally fallen into a peaceful sleep. Dinner was not until nine, so Mary pushed her books aside and lay down to rest.

Claire, however, was far from sleep and full of thoughts and feelings she made no effort to restrain.

She sat in her room in the early evening at a small writing desk wearing a long dark green dressing gown, her dark hair in disarray. The room cold. The fire burnt low hours ago.

Claire took no notice.

Bent over her diary, the India ink from the quill pen splotching the page and staining her fingers, she wrote with a pen too full and too hard pressed.

"She wants them both! I know it! I have seen her looking at Him. That pale thing with her books. But He will be mine! If only She not interfere! She Will Not Dare once I tell them of the Babe! And then I shall be Lady Byron, and She, not even married! If I cannot have Him—I will tear Shelley out of her arms—by the root! I know I have influence there—but I must, I Will—have HIM!"

Claire looked up, beyond the circle of candle light she wrote within, staring into the cold darkening room.

With a sharp desperate cry, she flung the pen into a far corner, and laying her head down in her arms sobbed desolately.

The Villa Diodati

TWENTY

TWO BUSY MEN

That same afternoon, Byron and Shelley sailed on Lake Geneva, enjoying themselves immensely, until a sudden wind turned the lake into such choppy swells, they had to fight to keep the small ship from capsizing.

Later, that evening, the four of them sat down to dinner. Byron's doctor, Polidori, having sprained his ankle, dined alone in his room.

At table, Byron and Shelley related their harrowing escape from the sudden squall, as if it were a boyish adventure.

Mary listened, assuring herself that she was put off by Byron's excessive nature.

Claire brooded, her thoughts colliding like angry wasps.

After dinner, Byron led them all into the library.

He was bored, he told himself, yet, if he were entirely honest, wasn't his interest provoked by Shelley's little Mary Godwin? She was pretty, but awfully quiet, somewhat mousey, not the sort he was attracted to, so this mysterious *frisson* he felt between them, puzzled him. Also, she would never answer his questions, and he found that damned annoying!

The library of the Villa Diodati was a grand room on the ground floor, its walls lined with a collection of books covered in tooled Moroccan leather, cosseted within cabinets of mahogany and leaded glass.

The tall mullioned windows overlooked Lake Geneva where the sun had set hours ago gleaming like a ruby amid the snowy mountain peaks that shone as if crowned with diamonds.

To the south, stood acres of dark primeval forest. An ancient overgrown vineyard rambled amiably nearby, nearly hidden in the rosy violet veils of twilight, as night drew near.

The library's stone floors were pleasingly warmed by Persian rugs, the windows hung with floor length silk panels. Above the fireplace, a wavy mirror rose to the ceiling reflecting the candlelight, rich furnishings, and the colorful company entering the room. At either end of the mantle, a replica of the Egyptian Sphinx ruled.

In all, whomever decorated the room had done so in the current fashion of 1816 for all things Classical and Egyptian.

A clock on the mantle chimed the late hour, as Shelley made himself comfortable on the couch and continued the dinner conversation. "I, for one, uphold the Banner of Free Love. After all, to the pure all things are pure. What do you say, Byron?"

Lord Byron remained standing, and finished his glass of wine before answering. "I hold a more conservative stance. When it comes to relations with the fair sex, I revere, chastity."

Fair words, Mary thought, but it is considered more than rumor that you and your half-sister are to have a child. And what of poor Claire?

"But love must be free!" proclaimed Shelley, excited by his own views.

"Evil exists and evil is sin," Byron proclaimed.

Mary wondered if this was not a remark to do with her, as yet unmarried to Shelley. Uneasily, her hand fluttered to her hair to smooth any loosened strand.

Claire seethed, pacing the room.

Look at her! Straightening and neatening herself. Well, m'lady, whatever it is he says he is, he don't like it neat!

"But Beauty, Byron, Beauty!" exclaimed Shelley.

Byron's answering laugh was more like a bark. "Oh yes, Cain's contempt had great Beauty!"

Mary was bewildered. His thoughts led one on a path that he obscured at every turn. He was dangerous. Dangerous and terribly handsome. Handsome and dangerously wild. Like a storm. A red gold storm with green eyes. She rose from her chair and went over to the fire.

Did she move to escape the sight of him, or to draw attention to herself? She did not know.

"What would life be without a fine evening on the lake, the beauty of the stars, and of a woman's eyes?" Shelley nearly sang, his voice quivering with emotion.

"Well, now, it's nice to be appreciated." Claire sat next to Shelley on the settee and wiped his perspiring brow with her handkerchief, desperate not to be left out.

Mary sat in a chair, annoyed with Percy's equating of women and stars and lakes.

Claire rose from the settee and moved toward Byron but he reached for a book and limped quickly away from her.

Adrift in the center of the room, Claire flew to Mary.

"Sometimes they talk so much nonsense, don't they, Mary?"

For once, Mary agreed with Claire, but she was too unsettled by feelings stirred by the older poet to respond, so Claire returned to Shelley.

"Lakes and stars, Percy? How am I like them?"

Shelley bent his mouth close to Claire's ear and whispered his reply.

"Why that's perfectly lovely, Percy!" Claire proclaimed to the room. But in a whisper, "Percy, why does he pay me no attention?"

"Do not mind him Claire. Do not mind any of us."

Claire was not soothed by Shelley's advice. He meant well, but was he blind? She had an eye in her head, and she had watched Byron and Mary all night. Claire bit her full lovely lower lip. They smell good to each other and they don't even know it! Turning her back on them, she renewed her attentions to Shelley.

Byron began to stoke the fire, adding logs, continuing to add bits of wood and paper, adding more and more fuel to the growing fire. Shelley and Claire, *tête-à-tête*, took no notice. Only Mary observed the older poet's extravagant measures that would encourage an excessive fire. She watched him out of the corner of her eye and said nothing.

Byron, not certain she noticed his performance, and furious at being ignored, picked up a book from a table and sacrificed it to the flames.

Mary was appalled and increasingly wary. He had burnt a lovely old book, yet in so unobtrusive a manner, neither Claire nor Shelley had observed him.

Mary could not resist confronting him. "Who have you consigned to the flames, Lord Byron?"

"Who would you wish destroyed, Mrs. Shelley? Perhaps Milton?"

A faint color rose in Mary's cheek. The man knew she and Shelley were not married.

"He would not be my first victim, Byron." She would not call him Lord.

"Who then?" The Sixth Lord Byron of Newstead's green eyes glittered. His wild mane of red-gold hair gleamed in the fire light as he strode to her and leaned down over her, one arm on her chair, the other held behind him as if to restrain himself.

Ah, he thought, her cheeks flame. Not mousey after all.

Well, look at that! Claire burned, spying on them from across the room. Even the aristocracy gets the scent, eventually. Thought he would need a pack of his hounds to find her. Very cozy like, they are.

"Oh, Geordie!" cried Claire, using a pet name she had originated that Byron loathed. "Would you howl for us like a wolf, like you did that time? It gave me such chills!"

Mary thought, she goes too far. Claire was unpredictable, but Byron even more so.

Byron strode to Claire, lowered his head close to her face, his eyes cold and fixed upon her. "Who are you." Not a question, but the vicious assertion of her absolute noth-ingness to him. Claire felt as if she'd been slapped. His intention, precisely.

His face a mask of disgust, he limped across the room toward Mary, who rose immediately and drifted over to the fireplace. Byron watched her escape him for the moment.

Mary seated herself in a chair, near the fire, that seemed to have captured her full attention. Claire walked over to the windows gazing out at the darkness to hide her tears.

Byron poured two glasses of wine for Shelley and himself.

What a bloody farce this is, Claire thought, with him and her and myself dancing about the room and each other, and Percy blind to it all.

Not used to being ignored, Byron left Shelley and strode back across the room toward the fire. He bent down along the way and lifted a small table, broke it neatly over his knee, and fed it to the flames. The hungry fire leapt and lunged into the room, molten sparks flying.

Mary snatched the hem of her gown away from them.

"You illustrate my point exactly, Byron!" Shelley drawled, rather drunk by now, and falling off his chair, slid down to the rug with a thump.

Furious, Claire remained at the window turning her back on them all.

Alone for the first time, Byron and Mary's eyes met.

The clock chimed midnight and broke the spell.

Byron suggested they tell ghost stories. Drawn by the sudden change in Byron's humor and by a flirtatious glance he shot in her direction, Claire left the window and joined the others.

After an hour or so of ghostly tales, that left them all on a nervous edge, the wind that had been building gradually all evening suddenly increased in strength, battering the windows and billowing the silk panels.

Mary walked over to the windows to shut them properly, when all at once the room fell quiet.

Curious, she turned round. Byron and Shelley were whispering.

"What are you two plotting?" Claire asked.

"A surprise for you both—Our Finale for the Ladies!" Byron crowed.

Both men left the room for the hall, Shelley stumbling behind Byron, who paused before a window, and tore away the scarlet silken cords that held the drapery in place. At the door, the men drunkenly pulled on cloaks, falling against the walls and each other, Shelley giggling, Byron shouting and grabbing the freshly opened bottle of wine, they swept out the door, into the night, leaving the door banging in the wind.

After a few stunned moments, Mary went to close the door.

She spent a moment frowning at the cloak rack before she returned to Claire and the fire.

Claire saw Mary's puzzled look. "What is it?"

"They're wearing our cloaks!"

The clock struck the quarter hour since the men left when the door burst open, a cold wind gusting into the room, and Byron bellowing, "Ladies! Your finale has begun!"

Mary and Claire rose from their chairs to stare astonished at the two night creatures.

The scent of pine bounded into the library with them, primitive and heraldic at once. But it was the sight of the men that the women found most terrifying, strange, and barbaric.

Two men crowned with what looked like a brace of antlers fashioned from branches of pine, held in place with the scarlet cords, loomed silently in the dimly lit hall like princely changeling stags.

Their arms laden with pine boughs, their legs muddy to the knees, the lovely cloaks borrowed from the women, now torn, muddy remnants of the garments they once were.

The women instinctively drew back. Mary and Claire looked from one man to the other, then to each other, their expressions mirroring the palest of fears. These were not the men they knew.

Two muddy green men entered the room, one with fiery hair, bellowing; the other laughing shrilly capered about, a rope coiled over his shoulder. After a few moments of harrowing frolic, they made straight for the fire and dropped their burdens there.

The door slammed back and forth unheeded, until Mary shut it again on a night shot with lightening like ravaged lace.

"Ladies!" Byron bawled. "Are you ready for your finale?

The women stared.

Byron continued never expecting a reply. "For we have been busy men! Remiss in our duties to you. But we will make it up. We have made most particular and unusual preparations!"

Byron was in good form. No, Mary corrected herself, the man was extraordinary. Drunken, yet, high-priest.

Shelley seemed painfully excited, almost unbearably so, yet ecstatic, his eyes darting from Mary to Claire then back to Byron, in a burning ring of glimmering glances.

"Shelley, fetch the book we marked in secret before dinner. You see, Ladies, we have been long in preparation. Now the time has come!" And saying so, Byron howled like a wolf gone mad.

Claire gave a cry of terror and scurried behind a chair.

Shelley dutifully hastened to a trunk that stood in a shadowy corner of the room.

Byron grinning wickedly, Mary thought she had never seen a man look so pleased with himself.

If she hadn't been so overwhelmed by Byron she would have been worried by the feverish look of Shelley: his face unnaturally flushed, his eyes over bright, he was fetching for Byron like a lovesick hound.

Byron announced, "We two men have one tale between us, for you two maids!"

With a lascivious laugh Byron addressed the women, while Percy beamed, enthralled. Byron reached for a bottle of brandy and uncorking it drank deeply, managing to leer first at one woman and then the other.

"Ladies! Have you heard the history of *der Golem*?"

Mary and Claire looked at each other, both confused and increasingly frightened, neither of them able to rise to the manic *Carnivale* atmosphere the man imposed.

While Percy retrieved the book, the older poet strode to the door, opened it and bent down to retrieve two buckets. "We will require moss, and of course, we will be needing clay. Even God required clay!" Byron carried in the two buckets, kicked the door shut, then carried them to the fireplace.

Byron reached for the brandy and stood in front of the fire as if awaiting Percy's assistance, but in his face Mary observed a look of terrible absence. Slowly, his chin dropped to his chest, the brandy bottle barely clasped.

Shelley carried a large book to the lectern, the sorcerer's apprentice, awaiting instructions, entirely in the power of his mesmeric Lord of Night.

Mary closed her eyes and then opened them as if to awaken from a disturbing dream. Claire was full of fear at the strangeness that filled the room, rampant and unbound.

Byron's head suddenly jerked up off his chest with a movement not unlike that of a marionette suddenly animated shouted. "The ladies must have their finale!"

"Oh, they must!" Shelley cried out.

"Lord Byron, what do you mean by a Finale?" Mary ventured.

"What do you mean to do, Geordie?" Claire whined, gripping the arms of her chair, ready to bolt.

"No need for explanations now. Tonight, I have a taste to play Conjurer." At that, he threw the near empty brandy bottle into the fireplace, shattering the glass, oblivious of the danger of flying shards.

Claire began to cry. Mary watched Byron closely.

He stood before the fire, his red gold hair glowing wildly in a tangled curling mane, looking, Mary thought, like a mythic creature from a fairy tale. A lion's head sporting antlers of pine boughs, resting on the broad shoulders of a man's vigorous body pulsing with Dionysian energy.

Shelley opened the book to a previously appointed page. He had lost most of his antlers along the way.

Byron strode back to the door for a rick of branches and gathering the remaining boughs into his arms he carried them to the hearth and dropped them onto the floor.

Standing before the fire, Byron tore off his crown of antlers, ripped away the remaining tatters of Mary's cloak he'd worn, and removed his own muddily savaged rose velvet jacket. In his soft collar and full-sleeved white shirt beneath the leather vest he often wore, he rolled up his sleeves, and barely glanced at a chair before he threw himself into it.

Claire swore to herself she never wanted to see this insane man again!

Mary thought she had never seen such a magnificent animal.

TWENTY-ONE

FINALE FOR THE LADIES

"Byron!" an exuberant Percy announced. "We may begin!"

Lord Byron sat slouched in his chair, chin resting heavily on his palm, staring blindly into the fire. At the sound of Shelley's voice, his head jerked up, but his eyes looked empty and uncomprehending.

"Geordie?"

Claire's unwanted attention roused the poet, no longer playful as before. He scowled at her as he rose from his chair, then dragged a long heavy wooden table away from the wall. He lunged for the bottle on the sideboard and took a deep draught, setting it at the far end of the table, but within reach, his mood visibly improving. Standing behind the table, leaning on it with both hands, a sly alertness returned.

Leering at the women from beneath golden brows, he spoke in a low, sinister voice. "Ladies! We Bring You Your Finale!"

Grinning suggestively, he seemed to invite them to some dark mystery and succeeded in frightening them both. No small part of his intention.

Mary's head throbbed painfully. The time was now more than two hours past midnight, and the villa had grown quite chill as the fire died down to a crimson glow. Mary drew her shawl more closely about her, anxious, yet exceedingly intrigued.

Claire was annoyed and longing for this night to end. Yet, she could not leave, not while Byron emanated such an intoxicatingly strange excitement.

"Attend Ladies. Attend!" Byron's voice boomed, as he strode about the room selecting two burning candelabras and setting them at either end of the table before him. "We shall need your assistance! You will take part, won't you? You must!"

Mary and Claire were daring young women, yet tonight veered beyond any boundary either of them had known. They were both, however, for the moment, still game.

Other candles in the room had burned down half way. The library was a sea of darkness with islands of gleaming candlelight reflecting in the polished mahogany wainscoting and glass fronted bookshelves, brilliant in the mirror above the mantle. The embers in the fireplace gleamed. Candlelight flickered. The wax trickled and pooled.

Byron shattered the radiant silence. "We are modern men and women, are we not?" He challenged them all as he paced back and forth, slashing the air with his gestures. "We respect science and logic. But we are men and women with a body and soul, made of flesh and blood and spirit. Do any here deny this? Do any of you deny the Soul?

"Percy, you are a man of science. Do you deny your Immortal Soul this night?"

"No, Byron, not tonight," he grinned.

"And, Ladies. Do either of you have any doubts?"

"Not me," pledged Claire.

Silence.

"Mary?"

"Yes, Lord Byron, I have doubts. But I have faith as well."

"Ah, then we may begin, and what follows may remove your doubts."

What can he have in mind? Mary wondered.

"First, I assemble my devices. Tried and tested ones, I assure you.

"A Cup!" he cried, as he reached for the latch on a glass case that held treasured historic possessions the Villa's owners displayed. It was locked. Byron smashed the glass with his fist and Clare screamed. Mary stared at him appalled. Percy grinned and giggled.

He grasped a golden goblet and held it high before placing it on the table. "Now, a Pentacle!" He spun about and retrieved a decorative plate from the mantle. "And a Sword!" A glass cabinet displayed a collection of gleaming weapons. This was locked as well. Byron smashed the glass, with his bloody fist, laughing as he grabbed hold of the wooden lattice and wrenched the door open, breaking the lock, and choosing a sword.

Shelley gazed in adoration.

"And last, we must have a Wand!" he cried, his look at the three of them a fierce question.

Mary and Shelley turned to each other in bewilderment. Finally, Claire piped up, "The poker by the fire, Geordie, that is very like a wand."

"Excellent, my dear!" the poet sang out with a grimace only Claire would mistake for a smile.

Claire plumped like a proud hen.

Byron arranged his devices. The poker, he placed before him, the Sword, a space below. To his right he stood the golden goblet, to the left he positioned the plate.

"The Wand, for power. The Cup, for the fullness of emptiness. The Sword, for the union of opposites," he crooned, as he swung it once overhead, cupping his privates and smiling lewdly at the women. "And finally, the plate, our Pentacle, will mean as the circle without end—Eternity."

"Now, bring some ashes from the fire, Percy!"

His helper scurried drunkenly to obey.

With several handfuls of ashes, Byron made a mound in the open center of the gathered objects. With his forefinger in the mound of ashes he traced a cross.

"And now we shall need blood!"

Claire flinched. "Geordie, what for?" Her voice whined in terror.

Mary leaned forward. "Lord Byron," she asked quietly, "what do you hope to accomplish?"

"I hope, Mary, nay, I pray, Mary, to call forth—A Being—not of this world! We relished our ghost stories, did we not?

"Be brave, Ladies! Be Brave!"

Byron assumed much when he urged only the women to be brave. Percy had an interest in the Occult, but his temperament was not suited to such explorations. Emotionally high-strung, verging on the hysteric when excited, he crouched on a chair, staring at Byron.

"Percy and I," Byron crowed, "have researched and found various formulae, but it is our conclusion that it is neither the form nor content of a formula that is important. We have concluded, without prejudice or superstition, that it is the state of one's belief that is crucial!

"It is *the Strength of One's Desire* that creates a most particular Brain Wave that may act as a Key, opening a Portal to *Other Realms of Time and Space and Perception!*

"An ancient Greek Philosopher, Leucippus of Miletus, believed all matter was made up of an infinite number of particles too small for the eye to see. He called them atoms.

"I say, that perhaps all of life, all of these atoms are held together by Dream and Desire, by Hope and Faith and Belief. And that someday, science shall find itself the servant of the Heart!

"If so, there is then, the possibility, that Desire alone will open such a passage, that our Finale tonight, our summons, may succeed!

"Percy! You support me in this do you not?"

The younger poet came back to life. "Oh, yes! Antiquity supports our theory as well! The ancient Egyptians believed the heart the wellspring from which reality is born." While in awe of the older poet, and lacking the raw virile power of Byron, Percy's interests were quite parallel.

"This night we shall summon the Power of the Heart!" Byron thundered, as he ripped his shirt open, baring his chest and the gleaming red-gold hair that covered it. He strode to the glass case housing a collection of weapons, grasped a jeweled dirk, and returned to stand behind the table. There he held the knife before his glittering grey eyes, then tore into the flesh over his heart.

Claire shrieked. Mary gasped as if shot.

"But one must pay a price, Claire. By our actions we proclaim ourselves.

"Now!" Byron shouted, gouging himself again, "Now I am open, mind and body. Open and flooded with Desire!"

Staring at the bloody wound blooming on his chest like a gory rose, Claire pressed both hands against her mouth to stifle her screams.

Byron leaned forward, bleeding upon the mound of grey ashes.

Then raised a fist high above his head and crashed it down upon the table, making cup, plate, sword, and poker dance. He pounded the table with one fist and then the other like a drum, as he sought a rhythm that eluded him, until it claimed him.

Mary, Percy, and Claire united by Byron's primal cadence, and given the hour, the last vestiges of the fire and flickering candlelight, the nearly tribal agreement to evoke a Being not of this world worked upon them all.

When Byron abruptly stopped drumming they all held their breath, suspended, waiting.

"*Come now! We must Desire and Believe, and we must Work!* Percy, bring the branches! Mary and Claire, the moss! We must first shape the material form for the being, like a port for a ship."

Both Mary and Claire both frowned and stared as the two men began to work with the branches and coils of hemp.

"The rope, Percy! Pass me the rope! Here. Around to the back. Bind the branches in place. Here, again. And again! Yes, again!

"Ladies, we call upon you!"

As Mary and Claire worked with them, the bound branches assumed the form of a large grotesque man-like thing. Then Byron and Percy began applying the clay, working it in, as the women filled crevices the smaller branches had not with moss. Shelley cast ashes on the wet clay, as directed, while Byron, to the women's horror, opened his wound again, flinging his blood upon the Green Man in a bloody Baptism.

Mary, and then Claire, soon found themselves inserting smaller branches, patching with clay, adding the last bits of moss, with wonder, if not belief.

"You think we make some hapless thing, Ladies? A mere doll? Ah, perhaps we do, but we try for so much more!

Percy! It is time to read to them of *der Golem*! And, you shall be our Fool, Shelley."

Here Byron darted an aside to the ladies. "I mean no disrespect, only as in the Tarot, ladies, he shall conduct us as we walk off cliffs together. And I shall be the Conjurer, watch and see! Shelley, begin!"

The women seated themselves, their entire attention captured.

Shelley wiped his hands on the remnant of Claire's cloak that hung upon him. Then pulled the first of the large and dusty tomes toward him as he stood behind the smaller table as before a lectern and began to read.

"*Golem*," Shelley began, "is an ancient Hebrew word, meaning shapeless, or incompletely formed. Der *Golem*, refers to a man-like creature created by sacred ritual. The ancient formula for evoking *der Golem* was discovered about 1100 AD by initiates of the *Kabbala*, a metaphysical body of Hebrew knowledge, with particular reverence and belief in the intrinsic power of certain combinations of letters of the Hebraic alphabet."

Shelley read well. The candlelight flickering across his face. His intense interest sobered and calmed him considerably. "The Mystery of *der Golem*," he continued, "was first recorded by Moses le Leon de Espana in a work called *the Zohar*. In

1156, Eleazar of Worms recorded a secret formula for evoking *der Golem*. It is a great misfortune that the original formula was destroyed by those who believe that man is not meant to penetrate the secrets of their Creator."

Byron paced silently back and forth in front of the fire as Percy read.

"The Talmud Sanhedrin records a creature evoked by a Kabbalist named Raba, who sent his creature to a certain Rabbi Zera. The golem arrived but could not speak. Rabbi Zera commanded him to return to his creator and the thing obeyed."

Shelley closed this book, reached for another and read.

"Whoever possesses such magical powers can, at will, master matter."

Byron repeated, shouting, *"Whoever possesses such magical powers can, at will, master matter!*

"Magical powers! Is it possible there is a scientific explanation for such powers? Wouldn't that be marvelous! If we might transform the pattern of Leucippus' atoms, why a tree might become a man!

"We do not try for a golem this night. No, we try for so much more! We strive to unlock the door! We reach for the power to master matter and evoke, to call forth a living Being!

"The Strength of our Desire shall create the particular Brain Wave that shall act as key and open the portal to Other Realms. This is The Lost Formula! The Power of the Heart!

Mary began to follow his reasoning. Listening to Shelley read from scholarly texts had soothed her. And that a particular mind state or Brain Wave might open a passage to another Realm or Time was such an intriguing idea that she found her fears abate as her interest grew.

"Byron, are you suggesting, that if the nature of matter depends upon the particular arrangement of the atoms, and, if one gained the power to rearrange those patterns, and effect their numbers and kind, one might change straw into gold?"

"Bravo Mary! And more! Much more! Why not transform, by this rearrangement of the original pattern, the non-living into the living! Why not animate the lifeless?"

"Why ever would you want to do that, Geordie? And how by Gawd would you do it?"

Now Byron spoke quietly, yet with great force. "Shelley and I believe there is a way."

Both women listened spellbound. Fatigue had left them all.

"There exists an ancient history of belief," Byron continued, his eyes burning, "in *The Power to Work Wonders!* Oral tradition and written records make the claim over and over that a certain few in every era discovered the means to heal the sick, raise the dead, change bodily form, see the future, read another's mind, and even fly! Tonight, however, we call on other realms and await one who shall answer! An angel, a devil, a perfect stranger, we cannot know."

Claire crossed her arms over her slightly swelling stomach with impatient disgust. *The man's an ass, and he's mad if he thinks I'm going to believe that!*

"Ladies! Think of it! All manner of wonderful feats! Accomplished by few, witnessed by many. But so few attained these powers, today we consider such accounts fable or folklore.

"But what if these accounts are true? In light of the atoms of Leucippus of Miletus, they are at least plausible."

"But how would you do it, Geordie? Get them powers, I mean."

"There exists, only in fragments, unfortunately, a record of the methods used all through the ages to achieve such powers.

"A certain state of feeling and belief are necessary. A state of trance! Reached by such practices as beating a drum repeatedly, and quite often, the taking of spirits." Byron drank a deep draught from the glinting bottle, then visited upon them all a ferociously handsome grin.

"But most important, is *Desire, a most passionate Desire,* to break through the barrier of commonly held beliefs. That is essential!"

Mary was utterly fascinated by what Byron was suggesting.

Claire, however, stretched her arms and yawned, tucking her feet under her on her chair, resting her head against its high back, looking quite ready to fall asleep.

Byron threw himself into a chair and waved a hand at Shelley to continue. "Read that last bit, Percy."

Shelley read, his face flushed, his eyes burning. "In sixteenth century Prague, a Rabbi Low gave life to a Golem from a clay figure he had made, but had to destroy it when it ran amok killing and maiming all in its path.

"In the seventeenth century, Rabbi Judah Loew ben Bezabel gave life to a man made of clay, although its mind appeared exceedingly dim. However, one day, for no apparent reason, it went into a frenzy that led to the destruction of property and the grisly disfigurement of its creator, and finally, to its own ghastly death.

"The Ten Sefirot of the Kabbala, refer to ten spheres and vessels, and also to the Ten Holy Emanations: emanations of numbers active in the vitalization of the parts of *der Golem's* body. Connecting the spheres are twenty-two paths, Paths of Wisdom, which together form the Tree of Sefirot, or the Tree of Life."

Percy closed the book he read from and sat down.

Byron leapt from his chair striding back and forth, brow furrowed. "Of course, these bits and pieces of records, complex and esoteric as they are, appear to be the most complete and utter rubbish. Pure superstition! No one of our modern era would give the least credence to such accounts.

"Yet, Percy and I are not discouraged. We do not believe that such natural disbelief rules out the possibility of obtaining the result!

"For if the ancient Greek wrote true, if trees and stars and men are all made of the same substance, those infinitely small particles Leucippus called atoms, and if matter is distinguished by the nature of such atoms, well then, might one not transform the atoms of one substance to the pre-ordained nature of another and, as Mary said—change straw into gold?

"Certain tones and rhythms found in ritual and chants aid in arousing a certain depth or height of feeling and belief, and so may incite such transformation!"

Mary was deeply impressed. A wild extrapolation, true, but a brilliant deduction! Fabulously intriguing.

But Byron had only hinted at what he would now propose. "The Kabbala's reverence for number and arrangement, and their rather astounding success, if we may believe them, well, they were experimenting in the right direction. However, we will go further tonight!"

His words woke Claire from her daze in alarm.

"Geordie, why would you want to! I do not see why we should!"

"Each of us must contribute something," Percy announced, soundly ignoring Claire. "Each of us must do our part. Byron has given his blood. We three must give something of our own."

"Dashing to the hall and back, Byron returned carrying something. "I shall also give it my cloak! Stand back. And with that he whirled his long black cloak about the would be shoulders of the thing and fastened it in place with the brass closures. "There now. Better."

Percy and Mary cut locks of their hair with a small jeweled knife from a cabinet, and wove them into the evergreen branches about the head of the Tree Man. Close to it, Mary found the scent of the pine boughs, the wet clay, and the damp moss, nearly overpowering. Claire tucked her handkerchief into one of the bound bundles of pine branches that appeared to be an arm, but moved away from the thing quickly.

They all sensed an uncanny atmosphere emanate from the man-like thing, like a cold current that might pull them all down to the bottom of some reservoir of time where ancient mystery still lived, and breathed.

Byron slashed at his arm and drew more blood, dribbling it over the table, forming an Arabic numeral eight lying on its side, the symbol of eternity. Then, once more, he began beating the surface of the table as if it were a drum, but this time, softly. Percy began chanting the sacred Hebraic word, YOD-HE-VAU-HE.

Byron's drumming and Percy's chant soon made Mary feel as if she were floating beyond the border of time. This is an age-old scene, she mused. Men and women passing the night together beating a drum and chanting, wondering at the mysteries of life and death, of souls and magic. We have been speaking of such things since the beginning of time.

Claire sat frozen in her chair afraid.

Byron could barely feel his hands as he beat the table steadily, however, the wound in his chest ached painfully. Percy repeated the Hebraic holy word, his gaze darting about the room. This was not a healthy exuberance. Percy tended toward consumption and such late hours, drunken intoxication, and feverish overexcitement were really too much for him.

Byron gazed at Mary. Soon after he had begun the drumming, she slipped to the floor and beat softly upon the hearth stones. Only the faintest embers shone like pale rubies, providing scant warmth; the candles burning, a gleaming golden light.

The room near dawn was heavy with damp. Meeting Byron's intense gaze, Mary felt desire flood her loins like a river of fire.

Lost in the beat of their drumming, and in the mesmerizing drone of Shelley's chant, Byron and Mary gazed upon each other, their desire pooling as Eternal time reigned.

Suddenly, Shelley shrieked. Wildly distressed, he keened like a tortured animal. Byron and Mary, startled from their trance, stared at him. Mary rose to her feet, never having seen him so pale.

He's gone mad, was Byron's first thought. Percy gaped and moaned piteously, rocking back and forth, his face assuming a shocking grin followed fast by a tragic mask as he pointed across the room.

Gooseflesh crept along Mary's arms and neck, rifling her hair. She gasped for breath as the heavy scent of pine mingled with the acrid stench of burning iron flooded the room.

Claire screamed and tore at her hair. Byron and Mary stood rooted in silence staring at the wisps of smoke that rose sinuously among the branches of the Thing they had made. They watched incredulously as small green fires burst into flame. Despite Byron's talk, his face and Claire's reflected disbelief and then disgust as the branches took form before their eyes, surging vigorously with life.

The four of them stared as the wet clay and tree branches transformed. Thick clusters of golden crystals, like brilliant topaz, oozed like sap no longer from branches but from muscular golden limbs. Sentient beacons swaddled with moss, soon brushed aside, gleamed dripping with damp. There was a buzzing, a snapping, a wind stirring, and finally, the unmistakable sound of breathing.

The head slowly turned toward them.

Byron moaned. Claire screamed.

The eyes opened. It saw them.

"Kill it!" Claire shrieked, skittering about the room. "Kill it! Kill it!"

The gaze of the luminous golden eyes cast about the room.

Percy sobbed, scuttling on all fours into the farthest corner where he curled up into a gibbering bundle, laughing, crying, and clawing the floor.

The Thing moved slowly, one arm and then the other, as if deeply curious, discovering its form and the space it occupied.

Head turning, exploring the room. Its gaze alighted on Mary, then Byron, and Claire with frank interest.

How beautiful, Mary thought. How utterly lovely and astonishing! She felt no fear, only awe, and a profound wonderment. Filled with delight, she smiled in utter rapture.

Byron growled. "It must be destroyed!" The horror of their

effort had instantly sobered his mind, if not his body. A burning hatred for the unnatural coursed through him as he reached for the sword and lunged toward his terrifying creation.

The head with opened eyes turned toward him.

Byron heard it breathe. Like a rustle of wind through countless thousands of years. A living labyrinth of time now couched in a human male body of muscular golden flesh.

Byron knew he may have called this Demon forth, but he had not created it. This was no mindless golem. The poet dropped the pitiful sword, staggered backward, drunkenly tripped and fell hitting his head on the stone floor where he sprawled unconscious.

Claire lurched forward and grabbed an iron poker leaning against the fireplace, but retreated with it to the farthest wall where Percy cowered. Only Mary remained standing where she had been, smiling softly at the Being who met her gaze.

"Mary! Are you mad? Let us go! Now!"

Mary ignored Claire and steadily returned the creature's gaze, having the peculiar feeling she was looking through a door, or was it a mirror? No, it was neither of these. Yet, something she might enter, or read. Something shocking was revealing itself, asserting some message, bodying forth—a current of vital energy welled up in this vigorous, vibrant space pulsing now between them. Life from another world!

Mary wondered at this Thing that with each moment resembled a living man more. It was certainly no longer only so many bundles of branches rudely tied together with rope. It was alive! A pale shining face had emerged. Golden eyes and a wide mouth with full golden lips. Hair wild and black. And forming among branches and moss and wet clay, under Byron's voluminous black velvet cloak, muscular golden arms and legs and a broad chest assumed human form. Towering over them. Perfect, yet incomplete as yet.

Oh, no. This was no mindless golem. None at all.

Mary took a small step toward It, hearing Claire cry out but as if from a great distance. The Being moved a step toward her, as well. She took another step, and then another. It did the same.

Inspired to offer a gesture of friendship to this wondrous Being, Mary raised her hands and lifted a golden circlet adorned with an intricate knot at its center, from her auburn hair. She then took another step forward, completely bridged the space between them, and offered it to the Being in her outstretched hand. At once, It leant toward her and accepted her gift taking it from her in one of its large golden hands, white light shimmering about the golden flesh, pale blue and silver light shooting forth from his finger tips and palms.

Byron moaned as he staggered upright. Seeing the thing so close to Mary he lunged for the nearest burning candelabra with murderous intent.

"No! Byron, no!" Mary tried to hold Byron back but the enraged poet pushed her aside to stalk the shockingly man-like Thing as it slowly stepped away from him. Byron lunged over the sofa, pushed chairs aside, finally dashing the burning candelabra at the vigilant Being, and in missing, threw the room into chaos as the flames climbed the heavy drapery.

The room in utter havoc, the evoked Being stood in stillness before the enraged man. Byron halted as if shot and fell to his knees beneath the deathless gaze. The Being took an interest in Byron, his gaze swept over the man taking the measure of the trappings these creatures clothed themselves with, and in the next instant, he stood before Byron wearing the poet's identical costume. The Being now clothed in boots very like Byron's, trousers, and the same poetical shirt and leather vest Lord Byron usually wore beneath the poet's cloak.

Mary shook her head in rapt amazement. *Who are you?*

At that, the Being turned to look at her.

She was certain It had read her mind.

Flames leaping about the room, with one last piercing look to Mary, the numinous Being leapt and crashed through the windows of the burning library, flew through the ancient vineyard, plunging into the forest in the grey light of dawn.

TWENTY-TWO

SOMETHING NOT RIGHT

Bending over the manuscript Julie read it as fast as she could decipher the feverish handwriting, fascinated, astonished, forgetting to breathe.

Finished, she read the entire manuscript again.

Then gathering the pages very gently to her, she held the pages close, with the strangest look on her face.

She didn't know how long she sat that way. Only that at some point she seemed to wake from a trance and realized she was hungry. She was about to go to the kitchen in search of a snack, when her gaze returned to the beautiful box. It tugged at her somehow. Like a magnet. Drawing her attention yet again. Until her eyes opened wide when the possibility hit her.

Heart pounding, she lay the manuscript aside, reached for the box and pulled out the second drawer. Again working the baseboard forward, getting slivers in her finger tips, until she sighed, as her reddening fingers again brushed papers.

And this time, as she drew them forth, found a bundle of letters.

Oh my God!

A smile spread across her face, although she stopped breathing for a moment, as her mind raced considering what she might have found.

The bundle of letters was bound with a ribbon but not tightly. So she could look through the bundle a bit and see that each one seemed to be addressed to Mary Shelley at different addresses: Italy, London, Scotland. She hadn't checked all of them yet.

And they were sent from several different European countries, too: from Italy, London, Germany, Scotland, and Norway.

Were they love letters? Written to Mary from Percy Shelley? Or, a lover? Of course they could be letters from a friend. They did all seem to be written by the same hand. The handwriting unmistakably the same. But they were hidden. And why would they be hidden by Mary, or anyone else, unless there was a very important reason to keep them secret.

Christ. Do not even think of opening them. Not even one!

These are historical! She shouldn't even be holding them in her hands. She should put them right back where she found them. No, since she'd already moved them, better just lay them in the box. And call someone who would know what to do with them. Like The Shelley Society.

She would call them at nine or ten or whenever they opened. It was nearly five in the morning now.

They would send someone over right away and they would take the letters, and the hidden manuscript with its own stunning, astonishing secret story that would soon become headlines across the internet and in every western paper if not others as well. And, of course, the Shelley Society would even take the rosewood box. Because, if authentic, they were all of historical value to be studied, written about, and preserved.

Well. Maybe someday they would.

But not now. Because Gran did not donate the manuscript to The Shelley Society. She passed it from grandmother to granddaughter, as it had been for almost two hundred years. And why was that?

Before now, no one had discovered the hidden letters and manuscript. Gran had given the box and what it held to her. It was a gift. Gran's last gift, and a family heirloom meant for her to inherit.

And maybe meant for her for a reason. And now that she had found the hidden letters and the hidden manuscript, she wondered if there was something else she should find. Another step she should take. Was this some sort of treasure hunt? Or mission?

Eyes wide, and taking a deep breath, she slipped the first envelope out from under the faded blue ribbon that held all the letters together.

Already opened, she slipped the first letter out of its envelope. Unfolding it, just to see who it was from, for now, looking for the signature.

And finding it, and reading it, she instinctively dropped the letter, letting it fall into her lap as she pulled away from it, trying to catch her breath. But she couldn't.

Even so, heart pounding, hands trembling, her cheeks burning, she dove back into the bundle of letters and opened every one of them. But long before she opened the last letter, she knew why the manuscript and especially the letters had been hidden.

Maybe even before she'd opened the first one.

The letters were hidden because they were written to Mary Shelley, and signed, *Your Demon.*

TWENTY-THREE

WHERE THERE'S SMOKE

After getting a few hours sleep, Julie caught the First Avenue bus uptown to Seventy-ninth Street, then the cross-town heading over to the West Side. But when the bus reached Fifth Avenue, she got off, deciding to walk across the park instead.

It was quarter to four. Their appointment for 4:30. Time enough to walk through the park. Maybe that would calm her down.

When she found the letters, she knew she needed to talk to someone. Someone with a background in science and the occult. Someone with a mind she could trust and respect. Someone open to the insanely impossible.

Ed was out of the question. Lorraine would be no help.

She only knew of one person who might see her and whose insight might help. Dr. Griffin Digger, the author of *Shaman and Sorcerers*, and *Ghosts, Magic, and Quantum Physics*.

Both books had been assigned reading for a course she'd taken on tribal religion and art. Both on the *Times'* Best Seller List, too, they'd read more like exciting novels, although he had charts, indexes, and voluminous notes for those who wanted to know more. The author's photo, taken in a jungle, was blurred. But according to the back cover, he was the director of the Hall of Tribal People at the Museum of Natural History in New York City.

He'd published a lot. So she pictured him kind of paunchy in a dusty office filled with papers and books. And extremely busy.

She decided not to call and risk being told by his secretary that he was unavailable. Instead, she emailed him directly. His email address was right there on the book flap. She only hoped the email was still good.

She kept it brief. Wrote that she had read those two books, and had a question she didn't believe would take much of his time. Might he meet with her?

He emailed her right back. He did come across as busy but also cordial, telling her to come to his office, giving her directions within the museum, and specifying a time, asking if it was convenient for her. Also asking her to state her question. With his long list of published books, he might be retirement age. Good. He'd be incredibly knowledgeable. She wrote back and thanked him.

She knew she'd been very lucky that he'd been kind enough to give her an appointment on no notice at all. She'd been even luckier when she emailed him back, thanking him and saying the time and place were most agreeable, but ignoring his request that she send along her question.

Perfect. She was about to make a fool of herself with a world class author and scholar, who also seemed to be a nice man. No wonder she was feeling on edge.

She knew the letters had to be a hoax. But why had the distinct feeling of dread and something like awe swept over her as she held the letters in her hands? Feelings she couldn't shake even now.

Julie followed the path that entered the park just south of the Metropolitan Museum of Art and walked west. It was amazing, she thought, once you entered Central Park, how soon you could imagine you were in a forest. Only the occasional bench or trash basket reminded her she was in the middle of New York City.

The only sounds that of the gulls overhead and their shrill distant cries.

It was a typical early December afternoon in New York City, chilly and damp and dreary. The early snowfall had melted away in the 40 degree weather. In Central Park, on a misty day like this one, the fallen golden oak and red maple leaves gleamed among those that had fallen earlier, already so many different shades of umber.

The park's beauty did not stop her from worrying about what she would say to this scientist, and expert on the occult.

At best, he would burst out laughing. Worst case scenario, he'd call Bellevue. Or, much more likely, just ask her to leave. So she walked along trying to think of the best way to tell him what she had found.

At first, she saw a few joggers, but they were heading for the track around the reservoir, or running toward the wider roadways. She soon found herself alone with her nervous thoughts.

The path narrowed and twisted, arching its back, following the sloping, even hilly land, so you would climb along until it plunged steeply into shadowy hollows.

Nearing the center of the park, she saw how wild it became here. Really a wood, now, overgrown and dark. And strangely quiet. Here, the older tarred paths buckled where roots strove through, up and out of the earth, cracking a cement curb if it got in their way, or growing up and over and around large boulders, they simply overwhelmed.

Julie took a deep breath and felt her muscles relax a little. She stopped walking for a moment to lay her hand against the crusty bark of a tree. What kind? She didn't know. Only by its size that it was an old tree, its thick roots rising above the ground, knotted and gnarled, and then, like dark sea serpents sinking silently, diving through tar and cement and cold hard ground as if they were water.

She took another deep breath, enjoying the musky fragrance of dry leaves and damp earth. It was lovely here. And peaceful. The leafless trees looked as if they had turned their attention quietly inward, to tend their inner life, a flame burning low in winter, shielded against the coming cold, guarded until spring.

The path pitched down into a deep and narrow hollow. It was darker here. Colder. She buttoned the top button of her black wool coat, pulled up the collar, shoved her gloved hands into the pockets and began walking again. She couldn't be late.

Julie saw no one, not even a squirrel. Hadn't heard a bird call, or dogs barking. The gulls were still with her although flying so high she no longer heard their cries.

Here, the path narrowed to a trail and the land rose on either side, as the path plunged and twisted deeper. At the bottom, trails crossed hers at every angle, the grass grew tall and wilder.

This had to be The Ramble. Acres of dense forest, wild and beautiful, but isolated. She walked faster.

She found herself walking at the bottom of a ravine where rooty fingers seemed to reach out for her, clawing their way out of the walls of damp earth that flanked the forlorn path. Long thin knotty branches, torn from the trees by the wind, were scattered everywhere, even larger branches here and there. Twigs lay about on the ground, looking like mysterious messages in the ancient language of runes.

A few steps further, Julie stopped suddenly.

Among fallen leaves and runic twigs, a crushed Camel cigarette pack, the kind her father smoked, and a memory of her father seized her, more real than the day.

Then, too, it had been a cold grey early winter afternoon.

They were flying a kite together. She must have been about five and bundled up, wearing mittens and muffler. Her father wore his grey overcoat, fedora, and maroon scarf. The kite string, wrapped around a branch, leapt in her hands, nearly all of the string played out.

The wind picked up and the kite began to toss and dive, so he put his cigarette between his lips while he steadied the bucking homemade kite he'd shown her how to make, its rag tail twisting, the thin paper snapping. She could smell the smoke from his cigarette and the burning tobacco, the scent of his Old Spice, too, the memory was so strong.

Memory? No. She smelled a burning cigarette right now. She whirled around. No one. Yet, it was as if someone were smoking a cigarette and standing right next to her!

It looked like she was alone. But she obviously wasn't.

Was someone stalking her? Julie felt fear lap a cold rough tongue along the back of her neck.

She told herself there must be a discarded cigarette still burning nearby. But she didn't see one.

She walked faster, then broke into a run. The smell of a burning cigarette became stronger. Panicked, she ran as fast as she could.

Until she stopped so fast she almost fell. Another one. An empty pack of Camels in a puddle in the middle of the path, the murky water glinting in the half light that filtered down to the floor of the hollow. It had lain so long in the water pooled in the crook of an exposed root, it had nearly lost its colors. The camel, pyramids and palms beckoned like a ghostly mirage.

The wind circling her, heavy with the scent of Old Spice, she stood still, not thinking a single thought, feeling disoriented and full of loss.

The cold damp began to penetrate, kissing her bones. A chill wind whipped through the trees. An unnatural silence reigned. She listened, but could hear nothing at all. Not even her own breath.

The circling gulls had disappeared.

And there was such a heavy fragrance of pine in the air now, too. At least that made sense. The path wandered through a grove of pine trees. Even so, she could still smell a burning cigarette, and the Old Spice.

You want to try a puff?

She had been sitting in his lap, only about three years old then, reaching for his cigarette and trying to catch the smoke, and, yes, she wanted to try. He let her. And she would never forget how the heat of the fire burned her lips, how the smoke slithered into her mouth and down her throat, then dropped its searing heavy coil into her chest.

She had coughed so hard and there had been that horrible burning taste in her mouth. Her father's wise strategy worked. She never touched a cigarette again.

Julie glanced at her watch. She'd better hurry. The ground rose here. She should be getting close to the West Side and out of the park soon.

Reaching the top of the rise, the path clear and wide, a few steps ahead, stood one of the old concrete water fountains. Few of them worked anymore. But water spurted from this one, and overflowed its brim. And a new, empty, pack of Camels lay in the pool of water encircling the fountain.

Three in a row.

She reached down for it, reaching through the silence, as if down through the years, as if the past were not past, as if for a holy relic, as if this pack of Camels belonged to her father.

Just then, a car's horn blared, a dog barked, and a filthy man exploded out of nearby bushes, his face a red mask, one hand working his crotch, his purple tongue lolling from side to side.

She bolted. Sympathy for the poor frightening man provoking her to decide she would not meet with nasty Ed tonight. There was enough strangeness in her life, and surely Dr. Griffin Digger would be able to answer her questions.

She ran up the path that led to a familiar weathered trellis, and there, across the traffic bound avenue the Museum of Natural History rose like the tomb of a long dead emperor.

TWENTY-FOUR

LA MUJER MYSTERIOSA

Down a dimly lit corridor of the Museum of Natural History, in a diorama within a hall temporarily closed to the public, a man appeared to be sleeping, but he was not.

. . . He was on The Other Side in a wind blown yurt, a tent made of caribou skin, battered by the roaring winds of the Siberian tundra.

He was leaping and whirling and banging a drum. The cries of birds streaming from his lips, his eyes like slits, but he could see, oh, he could see, such things!

Spirits of Death flew about the tent rifling his hair like a lovesick woman. The swarm of murderous spirits wore the same leering face—that of the enemy who had cursed the man on the bed of furs.

The shaman would cure his friend this night, or lose him forever.

Naked, save for a loincloth, taut muscles gilt with sweat, as if he had just left a bed of love, deep in ecstasy, he tossed his drum and it flew up through the smoke hole of the tent, flying into the night to lodge among the stars until he called for it again.

Then, as if struck by a blow, the shaman dropped to the frozen earthen floor of the yurt, eyes closed.

Slowly, a swirl of mist rose from the back of his head, curling like smoke in the frigid air, assuming the shape of the man. Twining about the tent's center pole, his soul rose to the top of the tent, slipping out through the smoke hole into the star flooded night.

He flew terribly fast, drawn by the cries of his friend's cursed soul imprisoned so deeply within an uncharted mystical geography. He flew over the red sand of the Chinese desert, over mountains crowned with ice, over the endless yellow steppes. A magpie could not have flown so far.

He must find his friend's imprisoned soul. If he failed, his friend would neither live nor die. His soul lost forever. His body left behind to rot.

The healer yearned to heal his suffering friend's soul shrieking in the limitless void, lost and despairing. The healer's heart and hands burned as he strove in his flight, reaching—

"... errrrr ... dggggggrrrrrrrrrrr ... "

... toward the desperate soul, bound in an unending darkness, crying out. He must find his friend! Then he would—

"ddrrrrr ... ddggggggrrrrrrrrrrrr!"

... lay his hands upon him and draw forth the evil, he—

"Dr. Digger! Are you all right?"

"Of ... course ... Paula ... "

... would challenge the ...

"Paula! Stop that! What ... is ... it?!"

Paula Wakefield, Dr. Griffin Digger's twenty-one year old research assistant, stooped down beside him in the diorama, had given his shoulder a hard shake.

"What is it? Your eyes were glassier than the stuffed yak down the hall. And they're not much better now!"

"Well . . . now . . . you have . . . my full . . . attention. . ." Digger ran one hand through his hair. Made an effort to sit up straight.

Couldn't, not yet.

Paula just shook her head.

"What is so . . . important, that you . . . disturbed me?"

Awkward, trying to unfold his long legs in this small place. Muscles cramped painfully. How long had he been out? He never knew. He tried to straighten his tie. Found his shirt unbuttoned.

"Disturbed you? Rescued you is more like it!"

Paula stooped in the tight space with the grace of a natural athlete, comfortable in her navy sweats and a white cotton t-shirt. Of course she was five, three—not six, two.

Wakefield was in her stocking feet, as was Digger. When inside the dioramas, staff left their shoes outside the camouflaged back door. Right now, she was trying to look into her thesis advisor's eyes even as she knew he was trying to avoid a closer look. They both knew this wasn't the first time she found him in this diorama to all appearances out cold.

"Rescued? Very dramatic, Paula. Perhaps theater, rather than anthropology, would suit you better."

"I was just—"

"And what did you think you were saving me from?" he snapped, feeling a sharp and bitter sense of loss.

"You were out cold—again!"

"I appreciate your concern, Paula, but you . . . exaggerate."

Dr. Digger's sharp tone didn't bother her. It only happened when you caught him—like this—and that didn't happen often.

The other grad students agreed, he was from another planet. True, but he was a genius! What did they expect?

He was only twenty-eight and had already written a ton of professional articles and books. Two of them had been New York Times' Best Sellers! He had an international reputation for his radical inter-disciplinary approach, with doctorates in anthropology, archaeology, and religion.

Oh, yeah, and quantum physics.

His lectures were broad ranging and eclectic and always packed. Especially debates. Students loved to watch him stagger his colleagues with his singular ability to interpret artifacts. He listened to them speak, he would say, if pressed. He shocked and appalled his cerebral systematic colleagues with his instinctive, physical approach, that bordered on the sensual, and mystical. Dr. Griffin Digger was prolific, brilliant, and a devoted interpreter and guardian of mystery.

And cute. Definitely cute.

"I can see the headlines now," Paula said, grinning:

"ARCHAEOLOGIST GOES NATIVE IN SHOP WINDOW!"

"Paula, the Museum of Natural History is not Macy's, and this is a diorama, not a shop window. Have you considered retail?"

"That's better. When you're sarcastic and picayune, I know you're your old self."

Old?

Today was Monday and the museum was open, however the Hall of Tribal People had been temporarily closed to the public while Griff and Paula reassembled the Siberian shaman exhibit, restoring the diorama to its original appearance, before its recent annual cleaning: arranging the manikins, their clothing, and the artifacts that contributed to the authentically contrived scene.

As director, Digger might have left the window dressing, as some smugly described it, to the graduate assistants employed by the department, but he always made time for this particular exhibit. After all, it only needed to be cleaned once a year and he enjoyed reassembling the exhibit. This is what he said, if anyone asked.

"You can go, Paula. I'll finish up."

"Okay, but you've got that appointment at 4:30?" She glanced quickly at her phone, "You've got twenty minutes."

The woman who hadn't said why she wanted to see him. "I don't know why I agreed to see her. We have so much to do before the benefit Friday."

"I know why."

"And I expect you are going to tell me." Gutsy girl. Pretty, too.

"When a Lady of Mystery requests your presence, what's a guy to do?"

"It has something to do with one of my books."

"Right. But listen, Dr. Digger, do you hear it?" Paula stood up, emoting stagily as she cupped her ear dramatically. *It's the Call of the Wild!*

"On your way—Paula, are you listening?"

"I hear and obey."

"Good. On your way, please take a look at the Australian Out-Back exhibit and see what the grad students have tried to slip past me this year?"

"I heard you didn't approve of their recent creative contribution."

"You mean the way they positioned the male and female manikins in the India exhibit?"

"Dr. Digger, it's all there in the Kama Sutra."

"The patrons of the museum do not come here for esoteric sex instruction, Paula." Griff didn't bother to suppress a smile.

Paula caught it and smiled back. "Might draw a larger crowd."

"True." Distracted, he gazed at the sick man lying beside him.

"The drums say you have no sense of humor, Dr. Digger."

"This is a museum, Paula, so will you please disillusion the children?"

"They're right, no sense of fun."

"Good night, Paula."

"I know you don't wear a watch, but you only have fifteen minutes until Mystery Woman!"

"Thank you, Paula. Oh, and please put a note on my door asking her to wait inside. And thank you for your help today. But get in early tomorrow. We still have a great deal to do before Friday."

"Bright and early. I promise!"

Outside the diorama's back door, Paula slipped into her running shoes and turned toward the Australian Out-Back diorama.

She considered herself lucky to be working for the renowned Dr. Griffin Digger. Even with his reputation, he never got stuffy. Also, he was fun to tease. He was so all work and no play! He had a great smile, if you were ever around for one of its rare appearances. Moody guy. A dreamer. But she loved it when he got going about his work.

His face exuberant, then serious by turns, he would cover the blackboard mapping out kinship lines, discuss and illustrate differences in blanket patterns, the data inherent in gnawed bones and worn out knives. Gently hold a ritual mask as he discussed meaning and function and respect.

When speaking of anything concerning anthropology, archaeology, and tribal people in particular—spiritual beliefs, clothing, the food they ate, the homes they built— his body moved with a heightened grace and energy. He had an eerie knack for assimilating wildly disparate facts, able to reach and convey an understanding of ancient life that eluded everyone else in the field. Every student and even his envious colleagues in the room were both enthralled and inspired.

When he was like that, the startling associations coming to him quickly as he made one after another unexpected connection, he was spectacular. And, Paula thought, incredibly attractive. So she couldn't help wondering about his personal life. Was he seeing anyone? The general consensus among the grad students was—no. Probably went with the territory. All that achievement and dedication. He gave her the impression of great energy under wraps. An intriguing thought.

Moody, brilliant, at times boyish, over six feet tall with broad shoulders, Dr. Digger's rich brown hair fell longer than would be expected given his position. High cheekbones and a handsome nose. His warm grey eyes inlaid with ebony and gold missed nothing.

A scholar with a wildness in him. Untamed, rough hewn. An unpredictable streak. He provoked most people before he said a word. He was mysterious. So people either tried to follow him around, or were solidly put off.

Paula sensed someone at war within. The methodical hard worker fighting a passionate nature?

Why was he alone? Or was he?

It was none of her business and she knew it. But she'd looked up his resume in the department's files and that's when she learned he was single, twenty-eight, and originally from northern Minnesota. A BA from the University of Chicago. PhD from Columbia. Post-grad, Yale. All on full scholarships and fellowships. A long list of publications; articles and books. Lectures all over the world: London, Paris, Berlin, Cairo, Mexico City, Tokyo, Peking. And PBS interviews with Bill Moyers and Charlie Rose.

Brilliant, accomplished, and attractive, courteous and thoughtful; and even with that occasional impatience of his, he was always professional. Never flirted with her. Unfortunately.

Instead, they talked anthropology, and he really listened to what she had to say. He declined her invitations for coffee or a quick dinner after work and always kept things between them teacher-student. Admirable. Too damn noble. Or, he just wasn't attracted to her. That seemed to be it. Fine. She would settle for learning all she could from him. She might hope, but she couldn't ask for more in a mentor.

With an unresigned sigh, she headed for the stairs and bumped into an old friend.

"Romeo! Que pas?"

When Paula left, Griff stretched his legs, propping himself up with some pillows elaborately embroidered and decorated with small mirrors.

Somehow, he had to be more careful. If anyone discovered his secret, doors would slam on him all over the world.

He had a good ten minutes before he had to head back to his office for his appointment with mystery woman. He needed a few minutes of quiet and solitude.

For now, he would try to forget about the benefit Thursday night. 'Hello, I'm Dr. Griffin Digger, Director of the Hall of Tribal People, and I am here tonight begging for your money to keep this dead zoo afloat.' That was not his take on the museum, but he had once overheard a child call it that and in moments when he resented certain aspects of his job he remembered the amusing dark humor.

While he was at it, he would try to forget the piles of paper work on his desk and the empty apartment that awaited him. The empty apartment and the empty life. And this was the best place he knew to forget all that. At least for a little while.

Sitting on the floor of a diorama that depicted a Mongolian goat herder's tent, propped up on the leather pillows glittering with tiny mirrors, leaning his elbow on a shelf of fake snow covered with furs, meant to create the illusion of a bed, he ran his fingers through the thick yak and fox furs,

. . . *gazing compassionately at the sick man lying on the bed . . . the man he had come to heal . . . his oldest friend.*

How quickly I am here again, he thought. It takes no time, no effort at all, anymore.

The ease of transition frightened him even as it thrilled him deeply.

Tonight, they were alone on an endless frozen tundra. He was here to cure the young man cursed by a rival. The shaman palmed the yellow quartz crystals to place upon the body of the young man: upon his stomach, his heart, wherever the evil lodged. He would withdraw the crystal at the proper moment and then the poison would withdraw. He would beat his drum, cure and fly. He—

"CRACK!CRACK!CRACK!" A quarter smacked against glass.

"Hey, Doc! You asleep or what?"

"I . . . was just . . . thinking, Romeo."

"Oh yeah?" The museum guard paced back and forth in front of the exhibit smoking a cigarillo.

"Dere's no air in dere, you know that? Eeets no healthy." He glanced over his shoulder and blew smoke at the No Smoking sign.

Romeo Corazón was short and stocky, with curly brown hair, and a complexion like coffee regular. He got along with everybody at the museum, except administration. They only had one complaint; they could never find him. He tended to wander off his assigned route. He told them it was his Latin blood.

By nature, a wanderer, Romeo left a trail of Polo cologne, danced every Saturday night until dawn, and carried a knife; a serious knife with an elegant bone handle. "Hey Doc, come on out of dere and les go down to them Indian poles and have us a little drink." The guard patted the bulge in his uniform jacket.

"How 'bout it?"

"I can't tonight. I've got an appointment right now."

"Oh, yeah. You right. You not supposed to keep the ladies waiting, Doc. 'Specially not La Mujer Mysteriosa! Heh, heh, heh."

"You've been talking to my so called loyal assistant, Ms. Wakefield."

"Oh yeah, Doc, Senorita Wakefield. She's a very pretty lady. You a lucky guy, only you dondt know it."

"I know Paula is pretty, Romeo."

"Dat's what I mean, you dondt! You know it here," Romeo pointed to his head, "but you dondt know it here," he said, pointing to his heart. "You other parts, I ain't too sure about," he laughed. Romeo took out his flask and took a sip. "Bottom line, she say to remine you, if it look like you was forgetting dat appoin'ment.

"To me it look like you was, but you no forget. Heh, heh, heh. Adios, Doc. Gotta go." Romeo sauntered down the hall to continue his rounds, singing softly "Alguna encantando noooche . . . " Griff shouted after him, "It's business, Romeo!"

"Next time, ok Doc? We go visit dose Indian poles. Strong stuff in dere. Anyway, I'm dyin' to know how you make out."

"Romeo!" Griff laughed. He always found Romeo's amiable irreverence immensely likable. The guard was already disappearing down one of the dimly lit corridors of the museum but Griffin could hear him call back, even as he could hear the echo of the guard's dancing feet.

"Don't worry, Doc, you weel know what to do . . . hee, hee, hee . . . Maybe!" Romeo's laughter echoed in the halls, fading as he took a turn down the next corridor dancing.

TWENTY-FIVE

WINGS OF SNOW

Romeo headed straight for the Great Totem Pole Hall.

Soaring well over sixty feet into the shadowy darkness overhead, from deeply carved and painted wood, the powerful forms of Raven, Bear, and Eagle emerged and crouched, embodying Spirits sacred to the Native American Indians of the Pacific Northwest.

Teeth bared, eyes piercing, sharp claws sweeping the air, they rose on each other's shoulders like a circus of gods.

The Great Totem Pole Hall was a popular room. People seemed drawn to it, as if they felt the presence of eternity calling to them through these masks of power.

Romeo knew these poles were full of power. He just stood there and soaked it up. After a few minutes he continued his rounds, finally arriving at his destination. He timed it so he got there every day about 4:30, just before closing.

Many in El Barrio might dream of Puerto Rico, or the beach for a vacation, but when Romeo Corazón dreamed, he dreamt of the snowy, windswept Arctic.

He had read the bronze plaque mounted on the wood paneling that framed the diorama's window many times before, but he read it again now. It was part of his ritual:

The Arctic: *Articus* (Latin), *Arktikos* (Greek) meaning of the bear, lying under the stellar constellation of *Ursa Major* and *Ursa Minor.*

While this diorama is by no means comprehensive in depicting all Arctic fauna, those included are representative of their species. The mature male Polar Bear, Ursus maritimus (550-1700 pounds) stands eight to twelve feet in height. The Ringed Seal, *Pusa hispida*, is dark grey, paler below, and rarely found outside the Arctic Region. The Snowy Owl, *Nyctea scandiaca*, is rare, found only in the extreme north. Its eyes, sulphur-yellow, its feet feathered to the claw."

Beyond the glass, within the diorama, the illusion of the wilds of the Arctic, a seemingly limitless landscape of ice and snow had been portrayed; including a drama of life and death. A magnificent yellow polar bear had hunted down a seal. On the plywood ice, covered with artificial snow, a museum artist had painted a splash of crimson. Overhead, against a cardboard sunset, a snowy owl flew with outstretched wings held in position by nearly invisible wires.

Romeo felt funny. His stomach a little upset. He took another swig of the rum, but it didn't help.

Then he saw him. *El Buho*, that big white owl starin' right at him. Maybe somethin' was going to happen again; one of his visions.

Life, she never the same, he thought. She show you somethin' different ever' time you look aroun'. She quite a Lady.

"Ok, what you gonna show me this time, Mamma. I'm ready fo' you!" Romeo reached inside his shirt and took hold of the beads of his *Collares*, for protection.

"Come to me," he whispered. "I am *Santero*, a man of power, but small, as all men of power, before *La Corazón de Mysteriosa*."

That *buho* was still lookin' at him. Shit.

"Santa Maria! What you want with dis Puerto Rican, eh? You want somethin' dats for sure. Come on. What is it? I ain't got all day, with all due respect, you un'erstand. Or maybe you got somethin' for me? The way you lookin at me, must be somethin."

He knew it was his fear that made him bait the god. But as Santero, he knew it was also known to work.

Romeo took a slow swig of the golden rum, then returned the small dark bottle to his jacket pocket. He reached back and took out his knife. "Beauty, I take you out tonight. Tonight, some kind of special." He placed the beautiful knife on the floor before the diorama, a gesture of submission. The long, black bone handle, covered with geometric carvings, was a holy knife. He could not say where it came from. He only knew he had awakened from his first trance in its possession. But even then, from the first moment, the knife seemed like an old friend, a companion of many years. Like he was married to the damn thing!

La Mysteriosa

Carefully, he observed everything about the diorama, his gaze returning to meet that of the owl. Finally, he couldn't look away. Nervous, he began to whistle and then to sing "Some Enchanted Evening," *pero en espanol*, in a slow hushed whisper.

"Alguno encantada noche . . . tu veras . . . un extranjero . . . "

He blinked his eyes. He could no longer focus. Good.

Rocking back and forth on his heels, his mouth slightly open, his eyes half closed, humming the song softly, he continued to rock slowly, back and forth, back and forth . . .

A light wind in the corridor ruffled his hair and *El Buho's* feathers.

"Hey, take it easy!" Romeo begged, even as he laughed a little. "It's been a while." He took another swig of rum.

In the diorama, thin veils of snow lifted, flew, and whirled. *El Buho's* wings began to rise and fall languidly, and then with full intent, circling until Romeo's knees bent, as he staggered under the full weight of the god when it stooped down upon him. Its razor sharp talons sank into the meat of his shoulders. The pain, excruciating. Like long knives sunk, all at once, deep into his flesh and muscle, anchoring in among his bones. He ground his teeth as he dropped to his knees, utterly crushed, body and soul.

He knelt for a time stripped of everything. He knelt in a silence so vast, in an emptiness so ruthless, if he were a younger man he might have prayed for death. As fully initiated Santero he could bear this perhaps a few moments longer.

When he thought he could take the pain no more, he found himself mercifully rising up. No, being lifted. His feet no longer touched the ground.

Far from the museum, the sharp talons held him possessively as the two of them, now one, rose into the sky. Prey and offering to this god's unfathomable soul, Romeo surrendered to the sheer power of Eternity's wild and untamable heart.

Behind the feathery mask of El Buho, Romeo blinked, shielding his eyes against the biting crystals of icy snow blowing about, as they flew above the bear and the seal. The white limitless expanse below glowed a bright pink splashed with gold as the sun set and the emerging blue and dusky violet shadows gamboled forth from icy bowers.

The great white owl shrieked as it rode the arctic winds above the gaudy sunset as the polar bear tore into his prey, healing his hunger. The seal's soul rose from his ravaged body and flew straight to the heart of the rising crescent moon. The owl screamed with pure joy.

Arctic winds blew fine snow about. The day's last vestiges of a rosy vermilion sunlight danced through a fine lace of twilight blue snowflakes as the silver moon rose slowly, with infinite patience and an ancient grace, and the wind whispered and shouted, sang and moaned, twisted, rolled, and snapped, whipping the sea, whirling the snow, taking big bites—and Romeo saw everything!

Flying in ecstasy until darkness descended and he found himself once more in his own body, in the dimly lit corridor, of the museum, standing in the blue light of the radiant diorama.

TWENTY-SIX

WHAT IF?

Out of the troll-ridden ghostly forest into an ornate tomb.

Julie had already been on edge and eerie coincidence didn't help. Three Camel cigarette packs, the kind her father smoked.

three in a row

The stench of a cigarette burning unseen.

following her

And the scent of Old Spice in the air, As if her father or his ghost was trying to get her attention.

And that was the beginning of insanity, wasn't it? When you begin to see significance where there is none; seeing a message in random commonplace events. The discarded cigarette packs might be coincidence, and their sense of personal importance superstition, but the scent of Old Spice in the air?

An hallucination, obviously. Apparently, therapy had not helped. Gin and tonic did not help. Nothing helped. *Christ.*

The guard at the door to the museum's lover level gave Julie a pass and directed her to the staff elevators.

It was no small comfort that once inside the museum and walking along the dimly lit corridors warm memories took the place of fear. She had come here as a child with her father.

Only one visit when she was about five.

She remembered holding his hand, trudging up the many steps to the museum's door, wanting to make a game of it and her father patiently not minding at all.

But he must have minded something. Why did he leave? And never come back.

What did I do, daddy? I won't do it again! Please come back!

Would she wonder and sorrow forever? Maybe.

Dimly lit, as it always was (and how she loved that), she remembered reaching up and taking his hand as they walked along these same corridors in their never-ending twilight, then pulling away and skipping ahead on her own, with the confidence of those who know they are loved and cared for, she had made a game of running away and then returning, and he in his overcoat, carrying his hat, the two of them had ambled happily through the maze of bright timeless vistas

Walking along the shadowy corridors, the luminous glow of the dioramas framed in heavy dark wood always made her think of a Jules Verne craft. The museum, an enchanted ship, or a baroque time-machine contrived by H. G. Wells. A strongly built exploratory vessel, elegantly designed, cruising smoothly through the seas of time. The dioramas, magical windows to look in on all the people and animals of the world.

Back then, when she was four, she distinctly remembered seeing tails twitch, eyes blink, and people smile as she waved and they waved back at her as they sailed by a family crouched around a fire just outside their cave at the dawn of mankind's story.

Or, drifting silently near a herd of wild animals, bringing you so close to the solid bulk of the wildebeests and zebra you could feel their enormous size in relation to your own, nearly run your hand along a lion's flanks and stroke their rippling muscles. You could almost see their hearts beating, their whiskers twitching. Feel the heat of the Savanna winds burning your cheek. The harsh wind of the steppes, the hot, dry air of the desert, the pungent earthy fragrance of North American woodland, with some imagination, these could all be yours.

If you were patient, watched carefully and listened, you might begin to hear the playful growls of the cubs, the soft whinnies of the foals; the patient grunts of the adults, the sneezes, the occasional cuff or kick. The roar of love, the wild cry of the kill. You were there, with them.

During that visit to the city with her father, he had also taken her cross-town to the Metropolitan Museum of Art where she especially remembered their exploring the Egyptian wing, and apart from the pretty jewelry and animal shaped vessels that caught her eye, she remembered standing with him and holding his hand before an exhibit of mummies.

Her father seemed to take a great interest in them. At the time, they looked like very big dolls to her, that came in beautiful boxes.

And now she was making her own little death dolls. No question. She was her father's daughter.

No question he had loved her. So why did he never come back?

For the first time, it suddenly occurred to her that maybe something had happened to him. Why had it taken her so long to imagine that? Maybe because she couldn't imagine or didn't want to even think anything bad could happen to him.

Christ.

4:20pm. Entering the staff elevator that would take her to Dr. Digger's office brought an end to her reveries and new theory. As the elevator door began to close she could feel the walls begin to move and close in on her. She folded her arms across her chest and felt her forehead bloom with perspiration. Her heart began to trip and beat faster. Her claustrophobia was a well-kept secret. Gran had never known, and she had never told Pearl. She told Lorraine any enclosure made her stomach feel queasy. But what she really felt was more like terror and doom. Knowing she was trapped. Knowing she was about to die. That these feelings made no sense made them even more terrifying.

Dr. Digger's office was on the topmost floor of the museum. By the time the elevator panel finally lit up the number six, the door opened just in time for her to rush out into the dark hall.

No cigarette smoke. No scent of Old Spice. 4:25.

Just as he mentioned, she found the narrow iron spiral staircase she would climb to reach his floor.

A note on his office door said he'd be back in a few minutes, and invited her to wait for him inside.

The door ajar. She entered.

The museum was over a hundred years old, the floor boards in his office wide planks darkened by age and at least a century of wax. Leaded glass windows bid the last of the early winter late afternoon sunlight enter through the nineteenth century panes that looked wavy with the palest green cast.

Just outside the windows, a deep stand of pine trees tossed in the wind, as if Central Park's dark enchanted forest had drifted near. Birds flew back and forth gathering for the evening. Thick ivy crept in the windows. Wind rustled the leaves.

The odd but charming thing about Dr. Digger's office was that it was round. Round, and overwhelmingly full of bright terrifyingly gorgeous sacred objects. That his office was round she attributed to its being the tower she'd often noticed from outside. The objects? Well, he was the director of the Hall of Tribal People and the author of books like *Shaman and Sorcerers,* and *Ghosts, Magic, and Quantum Physics.* So it all made perfect sense.

The curving wall, large oak desk, bookcases, and every available surface including the worn leather couch and the floor were crowded with archeological treasures. Spectacular objects of sacred magic.

Ordinarily, she would have been fascinated, but today, still shaken by Gran's death, mystified by the hidden manuscript, and most of all by the stunning signature on the letters, fresh from her haunting experience in the park, and a panic attack in the elevator, the riot of garish masks and tribal fetishes that leapt out at her jolted her.

It was like opening a room full of screaming souls demanding time take them back.

Power flooded the room. A Central American fertility goddess, a portion of a Haida totem pole with Raven staring at her and Bear sticking out his tongue; African masks; a carved wooden fetish figure of some kind of small mammal obsessively pierced with nails.

More masks, that looked like they were from the Far East. One with large, round black eyes, carved spiraling golden horns, a predatory beak with rows of sharp white teeth embellished with bright crimson. She wondered how he could work with these things around him all the time?

These living things.

For certainly they were alive, hissing, and roaring!

A foot tall carved ivory polar bear reared up on his hind legs, jaws opened wide, filled with tiny pointed yellow teeth. An old Navaho rug, woven in the traditional red, black, and white diamond pattern lay over the back of the leather couch. Axes, spears, and arrows hung on the walls and over the small fireplace. A large framed Chinese ink landscape of gorgeous trees, waterfalls and one sage meditating on a cliff, hung next to what looked like parchment covered with Mayan glyphs.

In a glass case, a Native American beaded breastplate and buckskin leggings. Leaning against the wall in a frame painted bright vermilion, dragons embroidered with gold thread.

Along a high shelf several statues of goddesses, symbols of the sacred feminine. One that had to be a repro of the prehistoric clay Venus of Willendorf all magnificent breasts and hips, a bronze Kwan-Yin: Chinese goddess of compassion; The Blessed Virgin Mary, her foot upon the snake's head; and the familiar Diana/Artemis goddess of the moon and the hunt. There were others she could not name that looked African, Hindu, Mexican, and Egyptian.

Oh my God! On the director's desk, in a wooden, glass fronted case, the mummy of a falcon, eyes painted in the Egyptian fashion, traces of paint still decorating the wrappings. She knelt to look at him more closely, mesmerized by this embodied hope in the eternal.

She got to her feet and gazed around the room. Any other day she would love everything here. But today, she had come for a scientific opinion and instead found she'd walked into a world ruled by magic.

She knew he had the credentials and seemed to love tribal art as she did, but could they talk? If she needed a sign, the large framed poster from Monet's water lily series behind his desk was a good one. She looked around for more clues.

Skis, poles, and what looked like an oar but with a paddle at both ends leaned against the wall.

Julie frowned. She didn't know this man at all. But she did know that what she had to say to him was going to sound completely crazy. Maybe she should leave.

The only other signs of him in the office were a long leather trench coat hung on a coat rack, a battered fedora, and a silky white scarf with fringe tossed on the couch. Steel rimmed sun glasses, with wrap around electric blue lenses on the desk. And this was December. Trench coat, fedora, scarf and sunglasses. He dressed like the Invisible Man.

Maybe she should leave now.

But something else caught her eye. She picked up what looked like an old photograph under glass in a silver freestanding frame. The photo looked like it dated from the early twentieth century from the look of the man's bathing suit. The original photo had been blurry, stained, and torn. She examined it closely, trying to figure out what was happening in the picture.

"Do you recognize him?"

Startled by the deep male voice that seemed to be coming from right behind her, Julie didn't turn around. Instead, she tried to sound as casual and at ease. Even though she suddenly found it hard to concentrate because he stood so near her she felt a warmth spread up her neck flaming her cheeks, and rollicking through her hair. This wasn't a panic attack, it was something worse, and far more pleasant.

She was blushing! What was wrong with her?

True, a man had not stood so close to her, well she couldn't remember when, but she didn't even know what he looked like. Although she somehow knew that if this was Dr. Griffin Digger he didn't sound like the paunchy academic she had imagined him to be. She could also smell cigar smoke on him, that she loved, and a lime scent, maybe from soap, and something indescribable that must be him.

She cleared her throat. "Uh, Not off-hand. I can barely see what's going on in the picture. Is he underwater?"

"Yes, he is. Keep looking. I'm sure you'll guess his secret."

He was standing so close he was breathing on her from above. He must be tall.

She felt nervous. Oh, he had just taken her by surprise, that's all. Now, who could this person in the photo be? She wasn't so sure she would guess his identity. He was wearing old fashioned swimming trunks down to his knees and floating awkwardly in a large square tank. His arms behind his back, he boasted a confident, if strained, grin.

When she guessed, she laughed. "Houdini!" Jubilant, she turned toward the voice she assumed belonged to Dr. Griffin Digger—who turned out to be one long tall drink of water.

Well, she'd known he was tall. His breath ruffling her hair, his deep voice coming from way over her head. Must be six-two or three.

"Bravo!"

When their eyes met, the fire that had scorched her face and neck now zoomed south, encircling her breasts, flooding her hips and thighs.

She dropped the picture, and when it hit the floor the glass cracked into several pieces but they didn't fall out of the frame.

Dr. Digger dove down just as she did, both of them bumping heads reaching for the framed photo, his other arm out to steady her, keeping her from falling into his lap.

"I'll get that," he said, as he picked up the picture frame, reached for her hand and pulled her upright, both trying unsuccessfully to ignore their far from standard introduction that surpassed any expectations either of them had.

When they both unconsciously rubbed their heads and caught the other at it, they both laughed.

"I'm so sorry!"

"Don't be. It's nothing. The photo is fine."

Desperately trying to change the subject, Julie blurted, "I, I've never seen a picture of him. Why—"

"I've just always liked the photo. It's difficult to know what is going on, and then you realize how important, well, it's a matter of life or death.

"Or," he added with a smile, "maybe I like it so much because he had a job even worse than mine: Trying to get people to give you their money to care for a building full of stuffed animals."

Julie smiled, recovering from her initial embarrassment. His easy going manner and easy sense of humor helped. But she was way off balance. This wasn't fair. He wasn't just good looking. He was handsome in a powerfully sensual, highly intelligent way.

His office filled with the vibrant color of dragons and magical masks was the perfect setting for this jewel of a man. Now she knew what they meant. He took her breath away.

And he was still standing only an inch away from her looking right at her with his very warm grey eyes flecked with chunks of gold and ebony.

Tall and broad shouldered. Thick dark brown hair worn a little longer than she'd expected. Like a medieval knight actually. He dressed like an academic with an edge. A dark grey form fitting crew neck sweater under a dark brown wool jacket with dark brown corduroy slacks. And boots. Black shined boots.

He returned the framed photo to his desk and held out his hand. "Allow me to introduce myself. I'm Dr. Griffin Digger and you are . . . ?" La Mujer Mysteriosa, no doubt.

"Julie Norwood, Dr. Digger. I love your collection. And again, I'm so sorry for—"

He shook his head to dismiss her need to apologize.

"Anything in particular you're drawn to?"

You? "Uh, the Falcon mummy, definitely. I'm an artist, and actually fabricating small mummies right now."

"Huh." It wasn't often anyone surprised him.

"I called—"

"Yes. Of course. Please, make yourself comfortable." He gestured toward a dark green leather visitor's chair, as he walked around his desk and lowered himself into his own dark green leather arm chair. The desk a sort of barrier. Protecting him from what?

For one thing, her aura. He'd had a momentary flash of it flooding the room, reflecting several conflicting feelings.

Her entire body blue, white light shooting out of her pores. Her head crowned with a swirling golden haze.

And, well, her breasts and hips, a deep pulsing crimson for just one or two glorious moments.

Griffin thought he might consider himself a man of some courage and self-reliance. He had done fieldwork for his dissertation in the jungles of the Yucatan. He could handle just about anything in a Central American jungle: jaguar, snakes, even *los brujos*.

But this young woman, which was why he'd had to turn away from her for a moment, earlier, when he placed the photo back on his desk, well. *He had never been so drawn to a woman so suddenly, so powerfully.*

Beautiful, yes. But something more. La Mujer Mysteriosa, indeed.

They were going into winter, but Julie Norwood smelled like spring. And from her aura it looked like she was attracted to him! Of course this was an unfair advantage of his. But women had so many! Beauty, intuition, emotional courage.

Get a grip. Remember who and what you are. And how that's an obstacle. Even if she were interested, he could not allow anything to happen between them. Not with his secret pasts, presents, and futures.

Digger cleared his throat. "When you called, you said you had found an old manuscript. How can I help?"

"Before I tell you, may I ask you something."

"Of course."

"Your field is religious beliefs of tribal people, right?"

"Generally speaking, yes. To be more specific, I've studied what most people would call the medicine men and women of the tribe, the healers; the magic men and women."

Griffin sat forward, his hands folded attentively. His eyebrows rose with interest as he peered intently at Julie but she missed all that.

Head bent, she knew this was her last chance to make some excuse, and run out of the room.

"Ms. Norwood? Have I answered your question?"

"Yes. Sorry. Please, call me Julie."

"All right, Julie. What can I do for you?"

Julie stared at him a beat. "I think I've found . . . the original manuscript . . . of Mary Shelley's Frankenstein."

"Oh? Well, that is an interesting find. Congratulations! Although, I don't understand why you called me. I never read the book, although, of course, I've seen the film with Karloff.

"And," Griff paused and smiled, "Young Frankenstein."

Julie smiled half-heartedly and nodded, but her eyes did not meet his.

He asked again, "Why did you come to me?"

In a small, quiet voice, as if confessing something she was ashamed of, Julie nearly whispered, "Because, I also found some letters."

"What sort of letters?"

"Letters written to Mary Shelley, and signed . . . Your Demon."

Griffin looked at the woman before him with a trace of sadness, searching her face for some sign of insanity. She looked tense, and now distraught, but otherwise seemed all right. But mentally disturbed people sometimes do.

Or was this some kind of joke? Would Paula go this far? He found the idea annoyed him immensely.

Pushing back his chair abruptly, he stood up. "Ms. Norwood, I really don't have time for this."

He was surprised at how irritated he felt. Because he felt so damn drawn to her, of course. "Unfortunately as director of the Hall of Tribal People, I have quite a busy week ahead of me." He could not believe he had just dragged out his title! Now he was more annoyed with himself.

He heard her whisper, "Sorry." In a somewhat louder whisper he heard her say, "You must think I'm insane."

Her lack of any defense disarmed him. Griffin leaned forward on his desk with both hands and asked gently. "Can you give me more information, or restate what you've just said? Are you telling me you're not playing some sort of joke?"

Julie looked up and held his gaze. "This is not a joke, Dr. Digger. But I shouldn't have come." She stood up and shouldered her bag. "I didn't expect you would believe me. Who would?"

She felt desperate, knowing she had just exhausted her only option. "It's just that I couldn't think of anyone else who I might talk to about them. I made a call to Harvard, about determining the authenticity of the manuscript, but that was before I read it. And before I found the letters."

The woman seemed genuinely distressed. "Ms. Norwood, Julie, please, sit down. Please?" Once she sat down again, Griffin did too. "They're a hoax, of course."

"That's just it. What would be the point? No one sold them to me. They were hidden. Someone didn't want these letters found!"

"If you don't mind telling me, how you did come to possess them?"

"My grandmother died recently—"

"I'm sorry."

Julie nodded and continued. "and the night before she passed away, she gave me an old beautifully carved wooden box.

"She told me that inside, I would find the original manuscript of Mary Shelley's *Frankenstein*, and that the box and the manuscript had been in our family since the eighteen-fifties, passed from grandmother to granddaughter, down to her and now to me."

"You had never heard of it before?"

"Never."

"Any reason to doubt what she told you?"

"I don't think so. She told me she was certain the manuscript was authentic. It was the last thing she told me before she went to sleep, the night she died."

Julie's face was so torn by confusion and grief that Griff believed her. Of course, the letters were a hoax, but she had nothing to do with it. He found himself enormously relieved. "Why would anyone keep the manuscript secret? The book was a great success."

"Not this one."

"I don't understand.

"I do now own the original manuscript, or think I do, but I also found a hidden one under the baseboard of one of the drawers. And that manuscript tells a different story."

Puzzled, Griff got up and walked to one of his windows facing the park. He stood there a moment. "How are they different?"

"First, since you haven't read *Frankenstein*, you should know that the novel is different from any of the movies."

Griff returned to his desk, but sat down on its edge, as he often did during lectures. Of course, sitting there brought him closer to her. "Go on."

"In the Karloff movie, as I'm sure you remember, the creature can only say a few words. He grunts, nods his head. Seems dull-witted and childlike with no experience of people or the world. Naive, but without a conscience. Quick to anger.

He doesn't know a thing about cause and effect, and being strong, he's dangerous, but not malicious.

"When he accidentally kills a child, the town people form an angry mob, chase him to a windmill, and burn it down with him inside."

Griff looked out a window. "I can still hear him screaming. How is her book different from the film?"

Julie got up and walked about the room as she spoke. "In Mary Shelley's novel, *Frankenstein*, we know what the creature is thinking, and he's not dull-witted, or childlike.

"He is intelligent, articulate, and in a lot of pain. He's been abandoned by his creator and he tells us about the lonely anguish he's feeling. He runs away from the laboratory where he was created and goes out into the world, where he learns to read and secretly observes people to learn how to live.

"He's filled with hope but people are so horrified at the sight of him, they run away. The creature begs his creator, Victor Frankenstein, to create a mate for him, promising they will go far away. Victor agrees, but later changes his mind. This betrayal fills the creature with a raging despair. He kills Victor's fiancée, and Victor's best friend.

"These are not mindless murders or accidental. The creature knows exactly what it's doing and feels no remorse. It murders for revenge. Blames the world for torturing him and teaching him to hate."

Julie dug in her bag. "I have a copy of the book with me. At one point, he says—'I am lonely and abhorred.' And here," Julie thumbed through the pages, "'Increase of knowledge only discovered to me more clearly what a wretched outcast I am.'"

Moved, Griff said, "'Lonely and abhorred.' Very sad."

"Yes. But after the murders, overwhelmed with grief and rage and a deep self loathing, the creature vows to kill himself in the Arctic wilderness. And that's the last we see of him in the book. Staggering across the ice, looking for a place to die. Intending to burn himself to death."

The only sound in the room, the wind rustling the ivy.

"The manuscript you found, tells a different story."

Julie returned to her chair. "Completely different. In this manuscript, there's no mad scientist stealing bodies from a graveyard. No using dead flesh to create a monster. The manuscript I inherited isn't a novel. It's titled: "FROM DARKNESS, A True Account by Mary Shelley," and it tells of a night when she, Percy Shelley, Lord Byron and Mary's half sister, Claire Clairmont evoked a Supernatural Being, Lord Byron leading them in an arcane ritual involving ancient symbols, hours of chanting, a bloody ritual, and . . . "

"And what?"

"And, what Byron referred to as The Power of Desire."

Griff nearly whispered, *"The Power of Desire."*

Julie nodded slowly. "The manuscript relates, and the letters I found substantiate, that contrary to what we thought happened that night in 1816 at the Villa Diodati in Geneva, Switzerland, Lord Byron, Percy Shelley, Mary Shelley, and her half-sister, Claire Clairmont attempted and succeeded in evoking a Supernatural Being that night. And that it left them just before dawn.

"The letters were written to Mary, from all over the world, and as I mentioned, signed, *'Your Demon.'*"

"Huh!" Griff felt like he'd been punched in the chest. He darted a look at Julie. She held his gaze.

"Dr. Digger," she said, leaning toward him, "I know how crazy this sounds but I don't think these letters are a joke, or a hoax. If Mary Shelley wrote them to herself, she must have gone mad."

Griff stared at her closely, his eyes intense.

"If the letters are authentic," she added quietly, but then her voice trailed off, wandering over the edge of the world as she knew it.

"I'll take a look at the manuscript and the letters, if you like. But again why did you come to me? You want someone who can authenticate the documents, don't you?"

"Two years ago, I took a course in Tribal Art and Religion at Hunter College. We read two of your books: *Shamans and Sorcerers*, and *Ghosts, Magic, and Quantum Physics*. What happened that night, described in the manuscript I inherited, involves what most people would call magic or sorcery, so, I thought of you, and your books.

"Your bio in the back of the books said you were director of the Hall of Tribal People at the Museum of Natural History here in New York and listed your email."

"I see."

"Dr. Digger, what if the letters aren't a hoax?"

"I don't follow you." Oh, didn't he. "What are you suggesting?" Make her say it. He had a good idea what she meant based on his own experiences. But he never shared that information. And he must stop her from following her line of thinking. It was far too dangerous for someone like her, who had no idea what she would be getting into.

"I'm not suggesting anything. I'm asking you some hard questions. And I want a serious answer!"

"All right."

"What if everything the hidden manuscript relates is true? What if they evoked an otherworldly being that night? What if the Being actually wrote those letters?"

Julie leaned closer, eyes wide. *"What if, It's still here?"*

He hated lying to her. But a lie could save her life. Other realities could be extremely dangerous territories. He must squash her interest beyond any doubt if he could.

He rose from his chair. And walked to his door, opening it, and obviously inviting her to leave. "I'm very sorry, but I believe the manuscript and the letters are a hoax. I strongly advise you not to be taken in by them.

"Now, if you'll excuse me, I am very busy."

Julie jumped out of her chair. And walked right up to him. "I came here to see you because of your books. Don't you stand up for what you write? In one of them you quote William James, something like, there's too much evidence to ignore the supernatural. But you want me to ignore it! And you're not even willing to consider it?"

"I don't doubt the supernatural, Julie. But I very much doubt that the manuscript and those letters are authentic."

"But why? And what if they are?"

"I'm terribly sorry but I really don't have time for this."

Shocked and feeling horribly let down, Julie stormed out the door, but before he could close it, she turned to face him and held it open. "You know what you are? You're a hypocrite and a fraud and, and a liar!"

That bridge thoroughly burned, she stalked down the hall, and pounded down the metal circular staircase so hard and fast it swung.

In front of the museum, Julie paced back and forth on the sidewalk in the dark, devastated and furious. Dr. Griffin Digger, author of *Shaman and Sorcerers*, and *Ghosts, Magic, and Quantum Physics* hadn't believed a word she said. Because he probably didn't believe a word he'd written!

And while he sounded and looked apologetic, he had thrown her out of his office rather than consider what she had to say.

Worse, now Ed was her only option. She would have to meet him for dinner tonight to see if she could learn anything from him.

She paused under a street lamp texting him. She would meet him at the restaurant.

TWENTY-SEVEN

THE PERSEPHONE PROJECT

Six weeks ago, Ed procured the female cub from a New Jersey mall.

When asked, it proudly told the procurer it was three years old.

Ed had opened the crate with a crowbar and installed it in the cage himself. Best not to involve Lyle.

It amused Ed to call this experiment The Persephone Project referring to the young Greek goddess Persephone kidnapped by the god Pluto, Lord of the Underworld. The project: a study in extreme isolation.

Awakening slowly from the ether-like drug her captor used when she was taken from the mall, regaining consciousness inside the dark iron chamber, she called out, "Mommy? Mommy?"

She heard footsteps, but they were not her mom's. Through the grate at the bottom of the cage, she saw a man's shoes and a bit of floor. The man's shoes looked like the crocodiles at the zoo!

Maybe this was a game. "Hello?" But the man did not speak to her. The shoes walked away.

She heard the door shut and locked. The room utterly silent.

In shock, she began to talk to herself in a sing-song voice, imitating her mother saying cheerily, "See? It's dark outside. Time to go to sleep."

Silence. She didn't know what should come next.

Then, "Mommy, sing to me? Mommy?"

Silence flooded the dark chamber.

In a frightened whisper, the young girl began singing. "You are my sunshine . . . my only sunshine . . ." But then her voice broke as she sobbed, "Mommy! Mommy! Mommy!" until she was shrieking. But no one came that night, or any night.

Ed was pleased that it had been such a healthy and attractive specimen. Ugliness, or any deformity, repelled him. It was a stroke of luck for him that he found it lovely.

Lucky for it too.

No matter. He would dispose of it soon. The tunnel leading to the river would prove convenient.

Thinking ahead, as he always did, he had another Pit of Despair built to adult specifications, now waiting under a tarp in a corner of his secret lab. Waiting for Julie.

The lab is dimly lit, but dark as a starless night inside the Pit of Despair.

She heard him come in. Saw the crocodile shoes through the grate at her feet. She asked politely, "Please put the light on?"

No contact, no response.

She asked again more loudly, "Please put the light on, please?"

Chittering little beast.

Ed filled the food tray and shoved it into the cage.

She looked down at it. Hard little grey things. They tasted like rocks. At first, she hadn't known they were food. The only thing the man had ever said to her was when he pushed the tray in the first time and noticed she'd only pushed them around. He'd said, "Eat." When she was hungry, she did. But they hurt her teeth.

She was hungry now, but she wanted Honey Nut Cheerios and banana and milk in her own Winnie the Pooh bowl. She shoved the food tray out and the dry pellets fell on the floor and on the man's shoes.

Ed stepped away from the cage. Brushed his shoes off with his handkerchief. Left and locked the door.

She pounded on the iron walls until tiring and hurting, she began to say her prayers. "God bless Mommy, God bless Daddy, and God bless . . . "

Silence. She couldn't remember her name anymore.

"God? Please put the light on?" Silence.

And then, the sound of a young child weeping.

All trouble aside, Ed was quite satisfied.

The odds were it would have grown up to be just another mall rat. Ed pursed his lips in his tight little smile. That was why, when he called it anything, he called it rat.

Rat had served its purpose, far beyond expectation. At first, he wondered if it would survive. There had been hours of shrieking and tears. The young are so emotional. But time and darkness and a punishing isolation had stopped all that.

It did not matter to him that he could never publish his results. He worked for the sheer elegant pleasure of control. If he were discovered, he would face imprisonment for life. Perhaps even be tried for murder. But he would not be discovered. For any day now her mind would simply give way.

And soon, very soon, he would have Julie.

In fact, tonight.

NET OF JEWELS

BOOK TWO

An Excerpt

FANGS I

Colin Donnelly, the day superintendent at The Scientific Studies Institute of New York hoped his boots wouldn't leak.

"Out of sight, out of mind," he grumbled. The river was taking the Sub-2 back, no doubt about it.

Jesus, Mary, and Joseph. It's cold down here! Even in his winter jacket he was beginning to feel it.

The Sub-2 was flooded. Had been for years. The water down here higher than it was last year, and some of the stuff floating around in it had to be unhealthy. Disgusting for sure. He'd have to throw these boots out. Would Accounts Payable reimburse him?

They'd laugh in his face. Then remind him no one asked him to take a stroll down here and wade around in this cesspool.

But he just didn't feel right about this area being so abandoned. Someone should know what's going on here.

And he would be that one, wouldn't he? Even if he couldn't remember the last time he got a raise.

So, at least once a year he came down. After a full day's work. Had to be almost six-thirty by now. He didn't bother looking at his watch.

He'd finish the tour and go home.

Something would have to be done about the Sub-2. And the state it was in, it better be soon. But they kept putting it off. What did they think? It was going to go away?

Donnelly noted crumbling walls, but watched his feet as he balanced on the planks laid on cinder blocks, that made a path over the flooded areas. The whole place wasn't under water because the floor dipped and rose and there were miles of tunnels and corridors beneath the Institute.

The light bulbs flickered. Old wiring. *Mother of God.* Of course, if a fire did get started here, nearly everything in the Sub 2 was too damp to kindle. But up near the ceiling, at the top of the metal shelving, some of that paper, given a spark, might be dry enough to burn.

Donnelly made note of the location.

The Sub-2 tunnels snaked around under the whole Institute, two levels below Founder's Hall and the libraries; offices and labs, above them.

If the Sub 2 went, everything went.

And still, nobody did anything about it. Thank God, it was off limits.

Donnelly reached in his pocket to answer his phone. That would be the wife. Now how did I know that?

"Where am I? I told you I was doing my check in the Sub 2 tonight."

"No, I'm not getting paid for this." She knows that. But

she has to bring it up. "I'll be home in an hour. It's only once a year. I gotta go!"

A little smile played across his stubborn Irish chin and five o'clock shadow. "Yeah. Me too." He slipped the phone in his jacket pocket and zipped it shut.

He was just about done and ready to leave, when he spotted some new serious water damage. He touched the wall and it crumbled like wet sand beneath his fingers, water weeping through. He was jotting down a description and location in the notebook he always carried when he heard a smooth metallic sound and looked up just in time to see an old battered metal bookcase swing away from the wall like magic.

What the—? And stranger still, behind it, a gleaming steel door that looked strong enough for a bank. When it began to open, Donnelly stepped back into a shadow, shoving his notebook inside his other jacket pocket.

The Sub 2 was completely off limits! And he was the only one with a key to the elevator! Or so he thought.

Ordinarily he would have called out right away. Questioning anybody down here. But that door and the camouflage shelving were so covert, the circumstances silenced and cautioned him.

And when Dr. Edward Henry strode out of that door, the hair on the back of Donnelly's neck stood up.

Dr. Henry was not on friendly terms with anyone at the Institute. Still, seeing him here, Colin would have greeted him and then warned him about the area, although the scientist had to know the Sub 2 was closed. It had been closed for decades!

So how did he get down here?

And what was he hiding behind that door?

He was about to say something, but decided not to. Chills were sweeping all over his body. *Jesus, Mary, and Joseph!* What was that about?

He watched as the scientist took his keys out to lock the door. This was beyond strange. What was he up to down here?

Dr. Henry was about to walk away when Donnelly stepped out of the shadow and called out a hello, as naturally as possible, given the cold waves of sweat breaking out all over his body. He asked the scientist, in the most polite way, what brought him down here.

Ed smiled, and invited him inside to see.

Every cell in Donnelly's body resisted going through that door.

But it was part of the job to know what was going on here. At least he saw it that way.

The scientist must have reclaimed one of the rooms for research purposes. They all wanted more space.

Dr. Henry told Colin he would show him the new project he was working on and Colin had to admit he was flattered. This would be some story for the wife tonight. And he was curious, too, but not for long.

As soon as he walked in and frowned when he saw the weird black iron cage, Ed swung the crowbar.

Available February 2013

BY JACQUELINE STIGMAN

THE FROM DARKNESS TRILOGY

BOOK ONE

AWAKENING
Available January 2013

BOOK TWO

NET OF JEWELS
Available February 2013

BOOK THREE

RETURNNNNNNN
Available March 2013

TAROT – TAROT

BOOK ONE

INHERITANCE
Available October 2013

For Further Information
http://www.jacquelinestigman.com

ACKNOWLEDGEMENTS

I thank Andrew Carnegie for all his libraries and the librarians who staff them. Especially my branch, the 67th Street Library in NYC. And my Librarian in Shining Armour, Frank Connolly—Yes, Griff will soon return your scarf. Although he asks if he can keep it just a little longer?

Thank you to these special teachers: Dr. John Bannon in Philosophy, and Dr. Stanley Clayes for reading Drama, both at Loyola in Chicago; Dr. Sydney Offit, and Marguerite Young, of The New School for classes in Creative Writing; Both Dr. Barbara Sproul for classes in Tribal Religion, Buddhism, and the Tau; and Dr. George Elder for a class in Evil at Hunter College, CUNY. Saul Zachary of Writer's Voice for Screenwriting, and author Frederick Tuten of City College for a class in Creative Writing.

Heart felt thanks to a reporter who once worked for one of Chicago's major newspapers, who came into the coffee shop every day where I was waitressing during my first two years of college and noticing I wrote poems on napkins when I got a chance, gave me my first thesaurus, that I still treasure.

Warm thanks and appreciation for the very generous support, info, suggestions, and classes given by the founders and members of the ITW International Thriller Writers at the Annual ThrillerFest Conference held each year in NYC, for readers and writers. Special thanks for their warm welcome, kindness, generosity, and support go to: David Morrell, Shane Gericke, M.J. Rose, RJ Ellory, Katherine Neville,

Gayle Lynds, Dakota Banks, Jon Land, Laura Joh Rowland, Don Helin, Rick Reed, and Leo & Linda Maloney.

For Dr. Karl Pribram a man of great compassion, kindness, and brilliance who kindly conversed with me about physics.

For Marian K. Chamberlain, founder of the National Council on Research for Women for her encouragement, interest, and our lunch at the Cosmopolitan Club.

Thanks to authors Jeff Carlson, Stephanie Cowell, Lev Grossman, and Hannah Tinti for info and writerly support. And special thanks to Tom Colgan for his encouragement.

For her elegant and awesome book design of FROM DARKNESS - Book One - Awakening—Interior and Cover— my respectful and warmest thanks to Gail Cross of Desert Isle Design, LLC.

Deep thanks to my first readers: Brave & enthusiastic Bob Johnson who read my very first draft and wrote helpful and encouraging comments all over it; Pat Bayley for her very thoughtful close reading, suggestions, and praise, for introducing me to the Kindle, and for her emails—"Send more book!" Miss you Patty! Thanks to Adam Dodway who made my day when he said, "What are you waiting for?"and to Evangeline Johns who said months after she'd read it, "You know, I still think about it!" To friend and neighbor, the Pesto Queen, Anna Grinjesch, for her incisive editorial insights, and for treating me to so many of her wonderful home cooked dinners! And to Joan Harris who was not much help with criticism at all, because all she would say is I love it! Send more! And I had to live with that. And Paton who went back to California but read my book and commented sagely first. Thanks to Richard Leighton, Jerry Matz and Steve Dhondt who encouraged me along the way. To Hazel Medina Matz for her warm encouragement. Miss you Hazel!

For their generous support that enabled me to keep working on my writing the following lent, bought, gave their spare, or repaired my computer for me; another gave me a printer. And still another bought me an air conditioner so I could survive a New York summer. And so I thank you all with great heartfelt gratitude because I could not have continued working without your help: Pauline Gilbert Bader, Roetta Collins, Diane Downs, Harry Wms. Harper, and Alvin Lotspeich.

Special thanks to Paul Deutschmann for his ongoing enthusiatic support, editiorial suggestions, and for researching and answering my questions regarding aviation.

Thanks to both Susan Murray and Jack McSherry, who help me when I'm not looking. And to Fanny Turschwell who bought lanterns for everyone on our floor during a blackout that enabled me to keep writing.

Thank you to friends and family who take an interest in my writing, asked how the book was going, and offered pep talks along the way: Catherine Anczerewicz, Sandy Bellinger, Ruth Botwinick, Angeline Brown, Ricardo Cavalcanti, Thena Cecil, Brendan Cecil, Irene Cecil, my godmother. Miss you! Jean Clarkson and Jon Stutz, Roetta Collins, Frank Connolly, John Conti and Rae Ramsey, Claudia and Frank Deutschmann, Frank Dulski, and the entire Dulski family, Howie Firth, Anna Grinjesch, Shane Gericke, Joan Harris, Leigh Harrison, Dr. Gerry Herman, Jay Hyams, Kay Gilbreath, Tara Huck and her mom, Carol Evans, my two Bodhisattvas, who both said, 'Just keep going!' Evangeline Johns, Greg Kachejian with his perfect cards for all occasions, sound advise, and great taste in candles. For Joanne Dado Kuksta, Larry Lewandowski Sr., Larry Lewandowski Jr., Joyce Matusek, Liz McCracken, Dr. Liz Meadows, Joan Nash, Don Newlove, Stewart Nicolson, Carol Ziccarelli Norbut, Fran Komendant O'Malley, Paul Oratofsky, Sandra Ritter, Dara Slack, Janelle Tiulentino, and Robert Weglarz. To Sue Bouder (also one of my first readers) and Bill and Zachary Pindar. Marie Gobby Polick, Marilyn Renk, Harris Whitley, Jacquelyn Whitesel, Mary Ellen Young, and Agnes Zientara, my other godmother.

Thank you to Zachary Pindar, again, Masanori Komatsu, Lindsay Harris, Jonathan Shew, Matthew Bellinger, Julia Clarkson Stutz, and Paul Deutschmann for all the fun we had and continue to have and the joy you all added to my life.

Not forgetting the furry four-footed people in my life: Danny III, Lamps, Blitzer, and Odibe for their warmth, caring, companionship, and fun they shared with those who were lucky to know them.

And a big shout out to Chicagoland to new friends Todd M. Paulson, Station Manager, and Bob Treciak, Paranormal Investigator and Host of WARG ~88.9 FM Monday night 9pm Radio Program: PARANORMAL RADIO ACTIVITY! Bob had me on his show September 24, 2012 to discuss paranormal experience and at every station break kindly announced that my book FROM DARKNESS would soon be available. Thank you Bob!

And thank you to Geraldo Rivera for having me on his Geraldo Rivera Show: GHOST BUSTERS.

Thanks to Big Red Production's Susan Stoltz for filming me twice in performance of Spoken Word.

And thanks to Flo Kennedy for having me interviewed by Peter Chelnik on The Flo Kennedy Show.

Special Remembrance and gratitude to my loving mother, Anne Weglarz Stigman and my loving father John Harold Stigman for giving me my chance.

To my grandparents: Dr. Charles Warren and Bernus Stigman, to Ludwig Weglarz, and to Nellie and Peter Borkowski.

And most especially to my brother Chuck Stigman and sister Bernice Stigman Lewandowski who I treasure, and for their loving support and while they live in Chicago they keep me informed about NYC and the world, and in general try to keep me grounded in this reality as I have tendencies to wander and live in books and movies, and 'elsewhere and otherwise.'

I am who I am today because of all of you. And I could not have written FROM DARKNESS without you.

Thank you all.

ABOUT THE AUTHOR

JACQUELINE STIGMAN grew up in Chicago, and now lives in New York City where she is working on her next novel of the supernatural.

Travels: Japan, Lapland, Norway, Orkney, and Scotland.

Connect with JACQUELINE STIGMAN Online
http://www.jacquelinestigman.com
http://www.facebook.com/jacqueline.stigman

Proof

Made in the USA
Charleston, SC
18 January 2013